Jake was speed

He hadn't heard ~~the~~ ~~birthday~~ song end but it obviously had, because people were applauding, men whistling, cries of 'Bravo!' were ringing in his ears. His mesmerised gaze travelled back up to Mel's face, just as she lifted her lashes.

And…*choong!*

Her eyes shot sizzling bolts of heat straight at him.

Nothing was suppressed in that look!

Amid the chaos of the moment, some deeply intuitive sense in Jake Devila told him his relationship with Mel Rossi had just been changed…for ever!

Initially a French/English teacher, **Emma Darcy** changed careers to computer programming before the happy demands of marriage and motherhood. Very much a people person, and always interested in relationships, she finds the world of romance fiction a thrilling one, and the challenge of creating her own cast of characters very addictive.

Recent titles by the same author:

TRADED TO THE SHEIKH
THE RAMIREZ BRIDE
THE SECRET BABY REVENGE

THE PLAYBOY BOSS'S CHOSEN BRIDE

BY
EMMA DARCY

MILLS & BOON®

All the characters in this book have no existence outside the imagination of the author, and have no relation whatsoever to anyone bearing the same name or names. They are not even distantly inspired by any individual known or unknown to the author, and all the incidents are pure invention.

First published in Great Britain 2006
Harlequin Mills & Boon Limited,
Eton House, 18-24 Paradise Road, Richmond, Surrey TW9 1SR

© Emma Darcy 2006

ISBN-13: 978 0 263 84857 1
ISBN-10:   0 263 84857 4

Set in Times Roman 10½ on 12¾ pt
01-1106-46788

Printed and bound in Spain
by Litografia Rosés, S.A., Barcelona

THE PLAYBOY BOSS'S CHOSEN BRIDE

CHAPTER ONE

JAKE DEVILA finished shaving and slapped some Platinum around his jaw, a cologne that had most women sniffing with interest. But not his prim and proper personal assistant, the indomitable Merlina Rossi. *She* invariably wrinkled her nose at it as though it was offensive.

He grinned to himself in the vanity mirror.

The idea that had come to him last night was sure to blast her usually impenetrable composure.

He really enjoyed getting to her, sitting back and watching the fireworks explode in her amber eyes. The eyes of a tiger, he'd often thought, and wondered if she'd ever unsheathe her claws and cut him to ribbons. Could be exciting—all that repressed passion bursting out, attacking him.

Unfortunately such a loss of control would probably lead to the end of the game and he didn't want that. Mel— she hated being called Mel and her endurance of it was another source of amusement to him—was his salt, a piquant contrast to the sugar of all the other women who sweetened his life. He'd miss her if she walked out on him. Still, he couldn't give up the exciting sense of brinkmanship with her. It was irresistible.

Must be close to eighteen months since she'd come to

work for him—the perfect Girl Friday, following his instructions to the letter, keeping his business and social diary on track at all times, fronting for him when he was committed elsewhere. He remembered now that it was this last requirement which had started the entertaining clash of wills.

The memory kept the grin on his face as he left the bathroom and walked into his dressing-room to select the clothes he'd wear today. Out of the many résumés he'd ploughed through to find the gem he was looking for, he'd picked Merlina Rossi's because she'd been P.A. to the editor of a teen magazine, which suggested she would be tuned into the teen market, by far the most profitable one for Jake's business, Signature Sounds.

She'd turned up to the interview in a loose-fitting black business suit, her long brown hair pulled back and held away from her face by severely placed tortoiseshell combs. She had a sensual look about her—a full-lipped mouth, large thickly lashed eyes, a golden tan to her skin, very curvy figure—probably her Italian genes coming to the fore, and she seemed intent on minimising their impact.

Not my type, Jake had thought. His preference ran to tall, slim, leggy blondes who specialised in *maximising* their impact, sophisticated women who aimed to win in the desirability stakes. He was perfectly happy to accommodate their female egos on that score, though he knew they always had their eye out for someone who would accommodate them even better. He'd lived in that world all his life, and observation and personal experience had taught him not to get emotionally attached to any of the women who walked through it.

'Enjoy them, my boy,' his grandfather had advised. 'The trick is not to take them too seriously or they'll take you.'

At the time his grandfather had been in the throes of his fourth divorce settlement and Jake remembered asking, 'Why do you keep marrying them?'

'Because I love weddings,' had come the blithe reply.

His grandfather could afford them, regardless of the end cost.

Jake didn't care to part with his own wealth so cavalierly. He'd worked for it and wasn't about to give any woman an easy ride with it just because she was sexually attractive. Work was something he did take seriously. He enjoyed being successful with his business and was very careful about selecting good people to help him maintain and build its success.

Merlina Rossi was in that category.

Definitely a prize find on many levels.

The initial interview with her had revealed she had a quick intelligence and would probably be very competent at doing whatever he required. However, the one thing that had niggled him was her strait-laced appearance. It was old-fashioned, out of step with his thinking, and if she wasn't flexible enough to change it...

'If you want the job, you'll have to dress for it,' he'd said. 'Your image is all wrong.'

It had been fascinating to see a flush rise up her long neck and flood into her cheeks, even more fascinating that she'd managed to keep her cool. 'It would be helpful if you'd explain what image you require,' she'd stated primly.

'Not that of a forty-year-old woman,' he'd tossed at her, his interest totally captivated by her determination to rise above any discomfort. Did Merlina Rossi have true grit? Was she a survivor against all odds? 'Your résumé says you're twenty-nine. Is that correct?'

'Yes.'

He'd strolled around his desk, propping himself against the front of it, his gaze deliberately sweeping her from head to foot as he explained, 'You should be dressing young, not old. We sell *Signature Sounds* to the owners of cell-phones and that market is predominantly young. If you're to represent me and my business you have to have street credibility.'

She'd calmly appraised him from head to foot. 'Does that mean jeans and T-shirt?'

It would have done, but the devil in him had been stirred by her slow, flat-eyed taking in of his appearance. 'No. That's fine for the guys who work for the company.' Including himself which she'd already noted. 'I would want you reflecting up-to-the-minute trends in young fashion. Jeans don't really make that statement for a woman since they're a constant. Let your hair down and show some flair, Ms Rossi.'

'My hair *is* down,' she'd said in a tight, challenging tone.

Which had instantly compelled Jake to take the point one challenging step further. 'Ah, yes, your hair. Might I suggest a more modern style? Something razor cut would be more in keeping with the image we want to present.'

Her cheeks had absolutely flamed and the devil in Jake had revelled in the fiery heat. Such a wonderfully tantalising question—would she play or would she fold?

'Are you asking for spikes?' she'd asked, the amber eyes spiking him as though he were a chicken she'd like to turn over a slow-burning fire.

Although tempted to fan the flames higher, Jake had realised a line was being drawn and she'd walk out if he went too far. *Down boy*, he'd told himself, deciding he could have a lot more fun with Ms Rossi down the road if she came on board with him.

'No.' He'd cocked his head, considering what might suit her well. 'Maybe a fringe and wispy bits framing your face and neck. Discuss it with your hairdresser. What you need is a trendy style to jazz yourself up. Understood?'

She made no comment on his suggestions, cutting straight to the major point. 'Are you offering me the job?'

'Yes. Providing that...'

'I fit the image.' She'd stood up and held out her hand to seal the agreement—all brisk business. 'Understood and agreed upon, Mr Devila. When do you want me to start?'

She had certainly socked it to him with the image, Jake reflected, putting on his usual casual gear for work. Mel Rossi was not only salt, but pepper, too—red-hot pepper when she put her mind to it.

She'd come strutting in that first day, looking very with it and sexy, her new hair-do swinging, the fringe on her high-heeled boots swinging, not to mention her curvaceous hips in the mini-skirt swinging, *and* the large ornate buckle of her low-slung belt had been centred just above the apex of her thighs, conjuring up images that had nothing at all to do with company business. Every guy who worked for him had been distracted.

But she'd just sailed around as though what she wore was nothing more nor less than a stipulated uniform, completely impersonal. She didn't flirt. There was no female wrangling, getting smitten guys to do any part of her job for her. She was Miss Efficiency. Had been from the word go. And Jake had to live with what he had brought upon himself.

So he had developed the game. Battle of the sexes. Exciting, exhilarating, sweetly satisfying. It could be said that Mel was the sex he had when he wasn't having sex. All in the mind and that was where it had to stay. However tempted he was at times, getting physical with her would be a big mistake. Any number of women were willing to share his bed. There was only one Mel Rossi and he didn't want to lose the delicious sizzle of the contest between them.

The idea that had come to him last night was sublime.

Mel wouldn't just sizzle, she would burn.

Jake could hardly wait for today's battle to be joined.

Merlina checked her appearance in the full-length mirror attached to the door of her clothes cupboard. Floaty, almost ankle-length skirts were *in*, a welcome change from the minis which invariably made her feel uncomfortably exposed to Jake Devila's endlessly provocative gaze. Not that this outfit would stop him from looking her over and smiling that smug little smile of his, taking personal credit for jazzing up her image. Personal satisfaction, too.

It always got under her skin but she never let it show. She held it firmly in her mind that she dressed for the job, not for him, though if she was completely honest with herself, she had become addicted to flouting her femininity in front of him, addicted to the sexual charge that simmered between them. And it wasn't good for her.

It dominated her life far too much, causing her to lose interest in other men. Here she was, looking down the barrel of being thirty years of age, and her current life was completely focused on a sexy devil who had absolutely no interest in getting married and having children. If ever a man epitomised the label of swinging bachelor it was Jake Devila. And he had all the attributes to go with it.

He was gorgeous; big brown eyes twinkling with wickedness, ridiculously long curly eyelashes that a woman would kill for, expressive eyebrows that worked like exclamation marks to whatever he was saying, very thick, fin-ger-inviting, wavy black hair, a strong straight nose, a strong square chin, a soft sensual and highly provocative mouth *and* dimples in his cheeks.

Dimples!

Merlina wished she wasn't so hopelessly fascinated by them.

The rest of him was eye candy, too. He had the physique of a prime athlete; broad shoulders, muscles where there should be muscles, not an ounce of flab anywhere, his whole body perfectly proportioned to his height, which was also perfect—tall without being too overpoweringly tall.

The man was born with not only a silver spoon in his mouth but a whole canteen of silver cutlery, and everything dished out to him on a silver platter. He came from a very wealthy family and he'd made millions himself with Signature Sounds, his own clever idea, tapping into pop culture. At thirty-five he had the world at his feet, includ-ing a stack of beautiful women—topline models, A-list so-cialites, television stars, all rolling through his social diary and no doubt his bed.

Despite meticulously carrying out her duties as his personal assistant, Merlina suspected Jake regarded her as his play-thing at work. He liked sparring with her. He liked baiting her. He liked giving her challenging tasks to see if she would perform as requested. The man was a playboy through and through. She knew it, yet couldn't stop herself from taking pride in successfully jumping through all his hoops and meeting his demands.

He couldn't defeat her.

No way.

She wouldn't let him.

Even so, she was more and more acutely aware of having become locked into an obsessive relationship with her boss—the exhilaration, the colour, the excitement he brought to her life. She admired the cleverness of his mind—the way he attacked business situations and fired enthusiastic creativity in his employees. His generosity in always giving recognition and rewards to those who came up with good marketable ideas also won her heartfelt approval.

Being with him was a constant buzz. There was so much about him she loved. *And hated.* Mostly because he wasn't ever going to view her as a partner he'd always want at his side. Not for everything. That truth was too clear for her to ignore. Or to hope for it to change. Jake Devila organised his life into games where he held the controlling hand, directing play, and the only game she had a part of was exclusive to the work-place.

Nevertheless, despite this knowledge and all her wary defences, he'd sucked her right into an emotional whirlpool and kept tugging her more deeply into it all the time. If she didn't climb out of it, she'd end up losing all respect for herself. Eighteen months with Jake Devila was really all she could afford. Her rational mind told her so.

Once she turned thirty, playtime had to be over and the serious business of finding a life partner for raising a family had to begin. She had only so many good child-bearing years, as her Italian papa kept reminding her, muttering that she had already wasted most of them in pursuing high-flying careers.

Her sisters were married with families.

Her brothers were married with families.

She wanted that, too…but on her own terms, not her family's. She had refused to let her father browbeat her into moving straight onto what he considered the appropriate life path for his daughters. Not until she was good and ready, she had vowed. There was no freedom in living up to parental expectations all the time. She had the right to be her own person and find out who she was by herself.

Except she wasn't her own person around Jake Devila.

She had to face up to that, put a stop to it and move on. Soon.

Or she'd fritter away what was left of her good child-bearing years, consumed by this dreadfully compulsive attraction to a man who'd never think of sharing the kind of future she really did want deep down in her heart.

'Merlina, what are you doing?' her sister called out. 'The pancakes I cooked for you are getting cold.'

'I told you I didn't want any, Sylvana,' she answered in exasperation, grabbing her handbag from the bed and heading out to the living area of her small apartment.

'You're too skinny. You need feeding up.'

Merlina gritted her teeth. Everyone in her family said that and she was fed up with hearing it. Just because they were all happy to be well padded did not make her skinny. She was simply thinner by comparison. The image she had to maintain could not be done with any excess weight and her figure was naturally curvy, which made following fashion trends challenging enough as it was.

'I had some yoghurt and fruit earlier on. I don't want anything else,' she stated, more than ready to say goodbye to the sister who'd come up to Sydney from Griffith to have laser treatment on her eyes, and who was staying overnight so she wouldn't feel rushed this morning.

Sylvana was seated at the kitchen servery, focused on feeding herself a stack of pancakes dripping with maple syrup. Already plump and working on getting plumper, Merlina thought as she said, 'I have to get going. I hope your short-sightedness gets fixed so you won't have to wear glasses any more.'

A fork loaded with pancake was halfway to her mouth which stayed gaping as she stared in shock at Merlina. 'You're not wearing *that* to work!'

That was obviously the outfit she'd so carefully put together; the long floaty skirt in a pretty floral pattern of greens and pinks, a woven pink-tan belt circling her hips, a dark green cropped cotton singlet, several long gold chains dangling from her neck, gold hoops in her ears and high-heeled dark green sandals on her feet.

Of course, her sister was wearing her usual respectable black: tailored pants right up to her waist and a long, loose T-shirt that covered up unsightly rolls of flesh.

'I'm expected to dress like this for my job, Sylvana,' she bit out, feeling her cheeks flame at the implied criticism.

'With bare skin around your waist?'

'It's a hipster skirt which happens to be very fashionable right now.'

'Your navel would show if the belt slipped a bit.'

'So what?'

'Papa would have a fit if he saw you displaying yourself like that in public.'

'This is the city, Sylvana. I don't have to answer to the Italian community in Griffith. No tongues are going to wag about me here, and yours had better not wag when you go home. Understood?'

Sylvana huffed. She was two years younger than Merlina, but being married and settled properly with a husband and young family apparently gave her the right to pick her wayward sister apart. 'It was bad enough when you got your beautiful hair cut in that raggedy fashion,' she started in again. 'I don't think this job is doing you any good.'

'It's *my* choice,' Merlina fired back, though she'd been coming to the same conclusion herself. For different reasons. 'I'm going now. Please make sure the door is locked when you leave. And give my love to the family when you get home.'

'Now you've got all snippy,' Sylvana threw at her.

'I wonder why,' flipped off her tongue as she passed the kitchen servery on her way to the front door.

'Wait!' Sylvana scuttled off the stool she'd been sitting on, rounded the bench and enveloped Merlina in a big squashy hug. 'I didn't mean to upset you. I just care about you, that's all.'

'Then please stop trying to put me in a box where I don't belong. We're different people. I like my hair style. I like my clothes. I like my job. So just let me be. Okay?' She kissed her sister on the cheek and eased away. 'Goodbye and good luck at the eye clinic.'

Sylvana said she was sorry for upsetting her and thanked her effusively for her hospitality as Merlina finally made good her escape.

Almost.

'Merlina, did you know you can see through that skirt? You need a petticoat on,' Sylvana called after her.

She waved and walked faster, rolling her eyes at her own scandalous behaviour in daring to break the rules of respectable dressing. All Jake Devila's doing, though he didn't know he'd done her a favour in stipulating his image requirements. Fulfilling them had actually been liberating, forcing her to shed inhibitions about showing off her body.

She'd always secretly envied girls who did, wishing she could feel as free about it.

Her job with Jake was the excuse, the permission, the goad to actually do what she'd wanted to do. Not that she went overboard with being sexually provocative. At least, she didn't think so. She wasn't wearing a G-string under this skirt. In fact, her hipster panties were far more modest than the bottom half of a bikini, which was something she'd never made the leap to wear, still sticking with a one-piece maillot for swimming.

Sylvana was just being stick-in-the-mud-Italian respectable. Merlina decided there was no reason to feel guilty about any of the changes she'd made to her appearance.

Having her hair cut had been a shock at first because it had always been long. Not that it was all short now, only the fringe and the wispy bits that feathered her face. The top layer ended just below her ears and actually waved because it wasn't carrying so much weight. The bottom layer was shoulder-length and it had a wave, too, making the style easy to keep looking good. It also definitely complemented her modern clothes.

Jake Devila had been the driving force behind her more modern makeover but this was her now, and she did like it. What's more, she wasn't going to revert to stodgy suits when she left him, though she might have to tone the pop culture clothes down a bit. Bare midriffs could be frowned upon in other work environments.

Whatever…the experience of working for Jake hadn't been all bad. In fact, it had been stimulating on many levels. Nevertheless, as she travelled on the train from Chatswood where she lived, to Milson's Point where Signature Sounds was located in a prime position over-

looking Sydney Harbour, Merlina kept telling herself it
had to end.

Soon.

Very soon.

CHAPTER TWO

LIFE could not be better, Jake happily decided, relaxing back into the large blue-grey leather chair which was perfectly contoured to give both comfort and support, lifting his feet onto his executive desk, linking his hands over his chest, his heart and mind feeling totally content with his world.

Mel, of course, disapproved of this unbusinesslike pose. Any minute now she would come in and stare at the soles of his shoes, refusing to greet him until he put them back down on the floor and sat up straight.

Mel had standards.

She'd make a good schoolmistress.

Or a nanny.

Which conjured up a number of enjoyable fantasies.

His gaze moved idly to the large picture window at the other end of his office. It gave a splendid view of the Sydney Harbour Bridge and he spotted a group of climbers making their way to the top of the great coathanger arch for the view from up there. They had a great morning for it—blue sky, bright sunshine, no smog. Something he should do one day, Jake thought—*climb every mountain...*

The tune of the old song hummed through his mind. He'd mention it to the boffins in the back rooms later this morning—get the disc jockeys and the sound mixers listening to it for application possibilities. There had to be a recording of it in their music library. Could be some part of it they could work up for the older generations who didn't like weird sound patterns for the call-tune on their cell-phones.

Now that he thought of it, that song came from the most popular musical of all time—*The Sound of Music* by Rodgers and Hammerstein. Big favourite with the oldies. Signature Sounds needed much more penetration on that market. Lot of spending power there not being tapped. Problem was, older people didn't use the Internet as readily as the kids, and that was where the sales were made. But if they could be reached through the kids...he had to get his computer guys thinking laterally.

Yep—got to climb every mountain.

Julie Andrews, who played the nun-nanny in the movie, was dancing around in his mind when the knock on his office door came and Mel waltzed in. She halted and stared at his shoes on the desk, just as Julie Andrews would have undoubtedly done when she played *Mary Poppins*, nose turning up in disdain at such an offence to proper standards of behaviour.

Respect, respect, respect, he silently chanted as he lifted his feet and swung them in a slow arc to the floor, grinning at Mel as he did so. She might act like a nanny but she sure didn't look like a nun! In fact, Julie Andrews was comprehensively wiped from his mind as the vision in front of him took instant priority.

'Ve...ry nice!' he remarked, taking in the artful combination of colours, the in-your-face display of feminine curves, and the tantalising eroticism of the long, swirling, almost see-through skirt. *Very hot*, he was thinking, but if he said that to Mel, she'd probably regard it as some form of sexual harassment and take him to the cleaners.

'Good morning, Jake,' she said primly, ignoring his comment on her new outfit.

She was probably ticking off in her mind that she'd met the *image* standard once again. Miss Efficiency never failed. But Jake had a challenge for her today.

'It is, indeed, a good morning, Mel,' he rolled out cheerfully. 'I've had some ideas. Got your notebook with you?' She was holding it in front of her like a shield, but Jake was just as good as she was at ignoring what he didn't want to acknowledge.

'Yes,' she answered, refusing to be baited, as usual.

Always being correct was a shield, too. Jake dearly wanted to blow that shield apart and get to some really vulnerable part of Mel Rossi—revelations of the woman within. 'Take a seat,' he invited with relish.

Only bucket armchairs in blue-grey leather were available so she had to settle in one of them. Jake suspected she would have preferred a straight-backed wooden kitchen chair. Instead of relaxing into the chair, she perched on the front of the seat and crossed her legs so she could prop her notebook on her uppermost knee.

The fullness of her skirt fell on either side, and Jake discovered, with satisfaction, that he actually could see her legs through the floaty floral fabric. Not that he'd never seen them before. It was simply more alluring to view them this way.

'I'm ready,' she declared—a warning that he should stop looking at her legs and get on with business.

Jake lifted his gaze to hers and smiled. 'Of course you

are,' he almost sang, overflowing with good humour. 'Ready, willing and waiting for the challenges I'm about to put to you today.'

And his smile grew into a huge grin.

I hate him.

The thought burned through Merlina's mind.

Jake Devila was never going to take her seriously as a person, or as a woman, or even as another human being who had feelings to be considered. He didn't care about her. He simply amused himself playing with her.

It was just plain crazy to be sitting here with her heart thumping like mad and her stomach all gooey because he had looked her over with very male appreciation, and his dimples were winking at her. That grin on his face was a sure sign he had diabolical mischief on his mind.

He rolled his chair forwards and lay his forearms on the desk, leaning towards her, his eyes twinkling, and she waited like a besotted fool to hear his brilliant ideas, then ran around like a maniac to meet whatever challenges he threw at her today.

I'm just a puppet on a string dancing to his tune, she told herself. Which probably wouldn't be so bad if it wasn't the only tune in her life but it was. And she had to move on from it. Her sense of self-worth insisted it was the only way to survive as an individual. But right now he had her locked into this moment, almost breathless with anticipation for what would come next.

'We need a think-tank meeting later this morning,' he said. 'All departments to attend. I want to throw around ideas for targeting the older market.'

It was a relief to hear him talking business. 'What time

for the meeting will I put on the memo?' she asked matter-of-factly.

'Eleven-fifteen. After morning coffee to get their brains active and before lunch so they can then chew over what's been discussed,' came the prompt reply.

'Right!' she said, making a note of the time.

'Get that memo out first, Mel.'

'Will do. Anything else before I attend to it?'

'Yes. Yes, there is,' he drawled, a wicked gleam in his eyes.

She concentrated on keeping her composure while waiting for him to elaborate.

He sat back in his chair, waving one hand casually as he said, 'My grandfather's birthday is coming up.'

So is mine, she thought.

'He'll be eighty.'

I'll be thirty.

'I want to do something special for him.'

He paused, watching her like a hawk, waiting to see which way its prey would jump.

Merlina patiently returned his gaze with limpid eyes, deliberately emptied of all emotion. She wasn't going to let him feed off her this morning! However, he paused for so long, she finally said, 'Are you asking me for suggestions?'

He laughed. 'Oh, I doubt very much you'd be tuned into what entertains my grandfather, Mel. He still drinks champagne at breakfast. In fact, when I was a little boy, he told me to call him Pop instead of Grandpa because he was such an expert at popping corks.'

Her tightly guarded mind had a malfunction and lost control of her tongue, letting wayward words roll off it. 'Perhaps you also have an equally pertinent reason for calling me Mel instead of Merlina.'

'Lethal weapon,' he rolled out, grinning at her again.

'I beg your pardon?'

'The movie, *Lethal Weapon*. Stars Mel Gibson.'

'You associate *me* with a male actor?'

Granted Mel Gibson always gave great performances in his movies, but he *was* a man, and how on earth could Jake Devila look her over the way he did if he thought of her as a man? Merlina wished she hadn't opened up on this sore point. She was just sick to death of being called Mel instead of her proper name. That particular thorn had been in her side throughout the whole period of her employment at Signature Sounds and obviously the urge to take it out and deal with it had got the better of her.

'Never mind,' she muttered, raising her guard again. 'I apologise for deviating from your grandfather's birthday. Please go on.'

'Believe me…the image I have of you has nothing to do with Mel Gibson's masculinity,' he said provocatively.

'I'm relieved to hear it.' Though she didn't want to hear any more. Clearly he was enjoying himself at her expense and frustrating him by not rising to the bait was the safer course. However, she couldn't resist a hit back before dismissing the subject. 'I was beginning to wonder how perverse your perception was. But again I apologise. Totally irrelevant. You were saying you wanted to do something special for your grandfather,' she reminded him with determined purpose.

'You don't want your curiosity satisfied?' he teased.

'I'm quite sure I don't,' she said dismissively.

'Because curiosity killed the cat and you won't risk it?' His eyes danced mockingly.

Her brain overheated. Retaliation steamed straight out

of it. 'When you were a little boy, Jake, someone should have taught you not to toy with cats. They have claws.'

'You're right,' he agreed. 'I should have had a nanny just like you, Mel. No doubt you would have turned me into a fine upstanding man.'

He was loving this exchange. Absolutely exulting in it.

She kept her mouth firmly shut. Not another word was going to escape her lips until he got back to business. *His* lips were twitching with amusement and his dimples were flashing devilment. She couldn't stop herself from glowering back at him but she did keep her mouth firmly shut.

He pointed a finger at her. 'Now that's just what I mean…why you remind me of Mel Gibson. Lots of pent-up energy that you know is going to explode into action when its fuse is lit.'

His eyes were dancing with excitement at the prospect of her losing her cool and blowing up. Merlina was sizzling inside but she wouldn't give him the satisfaction of a steaming reply. That would mean he'd won his point. She grimly maintained her dignity and he finally sighed his surrender to her brick wall defence.

'Right! To get back to my grandfather…'

Ah, yes, Merlina thought, still glowering. The champagne cork-popping Byron Devila was notorious for his numerous marriages, just about rivalling King Henry the Eighth on that score. Jake probably took after him in the playboy stakes. The only difference was his grandfather married his playthings. Probably a generational thing. It wouldn't have been so socially acceptable to have a string of temporary bed-partners in the years of *his* prime.

'…I want you to organise a cake.'

'A cake,' she repeated, tearing her smouldering gaze

from the twinkling mischief in his and assiduously writing
the word in her notebook.

'A very special cake. Eight tiers should do it,' he went
on. 'One for each decade of his life.'

Merlina wrote *8 tiers*. She thought it a bit excessive,
but...*hers not to reason why, hers but to do or die!*

'And I want eighty candles spread around the edge of
the tiers.'

'That's going to make it hard for him to blow them all
out,' she remarked.

'You'd be surprised how hale and hearty my grandfather is,' came the bland reply.

She flicked a derisive glance at him. 'Do you really
want to give his lungs such a demanding workout on his
birthday?'

He smiled. 'Good of you to care about him, Mel, but I
didn't mean for the candles to be real.'

'Just decorative candles? They're not to be lit?'

'Decorative, yes. Very decorative.'

She rolled her eyes and wrote *decorative only*.

'They won't be real, any more than the cake will be
real,' Jake said helpfully.

It didn't help. Merlina felt her mind moving towards
meltdown. Her hand tightened its grip on the solid reality
of her pen and very slowly she lifted her gaze from the
notebook on her knee, intent on staring her tormentor down
until he behaved himself as a proper boss should. 'Please
explain,' she said in a dead-pan voice.

He laughed, setting off fireworks in her head—fizzy
Roman candles and rockets that zoomed up and exploded.

She hated him, hated him, hated him.

Most of all, she hated how deeply he affected her.

Every cell in her body was jangling with awareness of him, the rippling joy in his laughter and the brilliant vivacity it brought to his all too handsome face.

I'm possessed by the devil, she thought, *and somehow, somehow, I have to expunge him from my consciousness and be totally free of him.*

'I'm afraid a call to Cakes for Special Occasions won't do it, Mel,' he drawled, having finally sobered up enough to speak.

She remained silent, waiting for appropriate instructions.

'You'll have to scout around, but I'm guessing that stage prop people could supply what I want.'

A fabricated cake, not a real one.

She refocussed her scattered mind and asked, 'What height do you have in mind and how wide should the bottom tier be?'

'I think six feet high should do it. And the top tier should be wide enough for a woman to emerge from the top of it.'

A woman!

'The tiers should graduate down to complement that width and provide steps for the woman to descend.'

He wanted a woman coming out of the cake!

'Inside, there should be some mechanism that opens the lid of the cake and slowly lifts the woman up to her full height above the top tier. Like a mini elevator.'

No doubt a woman in spangles and a G-string!

'And the cake should be on rollers so it can be wheeled out to my grandfather at the optimum moment.'

A gift of a woman to his playboy Pop!

'You're not writing any of this down, Mel,' he chided.

'It's being imprinted on my brain,' she answered truthfully.

'As long as you get it right.'

'Don't worry. I'll get it right.'

'Okay! Now the woman…'

Oh, yes, having unwrapped the decorative cake, what precisely was to emerge on cue?

'She has to be a blonde.'

Of course. Jake had obviously inherited his taste in blondes from his grandfather.

He grinned at her. 'And curvy like you, Mel. A Marilyn Monroe type.'

A treacherous thrill ran through her entire body. Jake was comparing her to the number one sex goddess of the movie world.

'Pop doesn't like his women skinny,' he went on, bursting her bubble.

Jake did like his women skinny. No doubt about that. Every one he took up with was pencil-thin. She had no chance at all of ever being taken up by him. Only her family thought she was skinny. Besides, she obviously had Mel Gibson's dangerous edge—*Lethal Weapon*—which wasn't sexy to a man who liked his women easy come, easy go, no complications.

'You should be able to hire one from the models who do photo shoots for Playboy-type magazines,' Jake suggested.

Merlina was goaded into speaking out. 'You realise this cake act is very old-hat stuff. And male chauvinism at its worst.'

'Absolutely,' he agreed, then waved his hand in an appeal for understanding. 'My grandfather still believes in marriage. Can you believe it?' He shook his head. 'Very old-hat. He'll love this. It's a scene from his favourite movie, made in 1966.'

She arched her eyebrows, aiming to get a hit at him. 'You seem to have movies on the brain this morning.'

'They mirror life,' he flipped back at her.

'Right!' Her teeth snapped. She ground them open enough to ask, 'What is the title of this movie? If I can find it in a video shop, I'll watch it in order to know exactly what you're describing.'

'It's called *How to Murder Your Wife*, starring Jack Lemmon and Virna Lisi.'

'I can understand why it's your grandfather's favourite movie,' she remarked with silky savagery. 'He's had seven wives so far, hasn't he?'

'Divorce from his seventh is about to come through,' Jake confirmed.

And how many playmates are you up to? Seventy-seven?

The problem was, she'd probably become the seventy-eighth if he focused that kind of interest on her. But he wouldn't. She knew he wasn't going to. Ever. Yet sometimes when he looked her over…

'There's no real murder in it,' Jake informed her. 'It's a comedy. Jake Lemmon is at a bachelor party and the cake is wheeled in. Virna Lisa pops out of it, their eyes meet, and *choong!*' He raised his arms in mock despair. 'It's the end of his swinging bachelor life.'

What she needed was some *choong*-power over Jake Devila. Before she rode off into the sunset of employment elsewhere, she would really like to sock it to him. Just once. Ending his swinging bachelor life was probably in the realm of pure fantasy. Maybe *choong*-power was, too, but…a wild idea was dawning in her mind, spreading light in the dark places she had nursed for the past eighteen months.

'Just for the record, in case I can't get a copy of the movie, what was Virna Lisi wearing when she emerged from the cake?' It couldn't have been too risqué, she thought. Not in an American film made back in the sixties.

'A bikini.' His brow wrinkled as he worked on the recollection.

A bikini...

To Merlina's whirling mind, it represented the final liberation, absolutely appropriate as the cut-off line to the Jake Devila experience which had served to break many conservative shackles from her upbringing. Wearing one in such a public spotlight would definitely be a mark of the confidence she would take with her when she left him. And her family would never know. It would just be for herself.

'I think it was made out of flowers. Very feminine,' he said.

She smiled, liking the description.

Quite acceptable.

And achievable.

Jake's frown deepened, his eyes sharply scanning hers, suspicious of her sudden good humour.

Her smile broadened as she uncrossed her legs and rose to her feet. 'Now that I've got the full picture, I'll go to work on it.'

He looked surprised at her willingness to proceed.

'What date is your grandfather's birthday?' she asked, since he hadn't yet given it.

'Next month. Fourteenth of February. St Valentine's Day.'

'Then maybe we should have the tiers of the cake shaped like hearts instead of circles,' she blithely suggested.

He jolted forward, leaning his forearms and his elbows on the desk again, his gaze trying to penetrate the workings of her mind. Apparently she'd given him a reaction he had not anticipated and Merlina felt giddily triumphant.

'St Valentine's Day is for lovers,' she trilled at him. 'Hearts and flowers. Agreed?'

He sighed and slumped back in his chair, sardonically muttering, 'Agreed. I take it you'll do this for me.'

'Oh, yes. I'll do it, Jake. Trust me. I'll do it.'

She was grinning as she sailed towards the door, gleefully knowing she'd beaten him at his own game this time. It didn't occur to her that she might have just been sucked more deeply into the whirlpool. Her exhilaration said she was on top of it, making her way out. With a bang!

'Don't forget the memo,' he threw at her grumpily.

She opened the door before looking back to resoundingly declare, 'I never forget.'

Jake broodingly watched her step out of his office and close the door behind her, punctuating her exit-line.

Somehow she'd turned the tables on him.

Mel Rossi was, without a doubt, the most provoking woman he'd ever met!

He'd had her simmering, even boiling, on the edge of blowing her top, then *Kaput!*—all sweetness and light, ready to play 'Happy Days Are Here Again.'

He'd have to come up with another idea because he refused to be defeated by her. He *was* going to break into the woman she was inside. It was just a matter of time.

CHAPTER THREE

JAKE had to hand it to his grandfather. He certainly knew how to throw a party. The old Vaucluse mansion and its magnificently landscaped grounds had been designed for hospitality on a grand scale and even at eighty—probably because he was eighty—Byron Devila was not about to give up his reputation of being the host with the most! He was still going strong and demonstrably proving it this afternoon.

The old man had not lost his pulling power, either. Not only was the crème of Sydney society here, but all *the establishment* from Melbourne, as well, along with a full complement of A-list celebrities. Jake noted that the Devila family had also come in force—four generations of them. He was running into relatives everywhere amongst the guests. Not that he was close to any of them—too many divorces fragmenting ties.

'Your grandfather is a real romantic, isn't he?' his partner for the party—Vanessa Hall of catwalk modelling fame—remarked, lifting her hand to smell the red rose attached to the white lace wrist-band she'd been presented with on arrival, along with all the other female guests.

Jake couldn't help smiling cynically as he answered, 'He knows the way to a woman's heart.'

Mel had been right about playing the St Valentine's Day card with the cake. His grandfather was using it big-time at this party. The florist who'd supplied the masses of roses arranged on pedestals everywhere had surely made a fortune from this one order. A silver dish of heart-shaped Belgium chocolates sat on the drinks trays being carried around by the waiters. French champagne bubbled in every glass. And a string orchestra was playing old love songs.

Vintage stuff on the romance front!

'Fantastic idea—having an English tea-party,' Vanessa burbled on. 'I just love dressing up like this. So feminine!'

With filmy hats and frills and flounces, and men in morning suits and top hats, it could have been a day at Royal Ascot, or Ladies' Day at Melbourne Cup week— definitely playtime for the rich and famous.

'You look radiantly beautiful in pink, Vanessa,' Jake rolled out, responding to the coquettish glance she fluttered at him.

Her blue eyes twinkled delight. Jake privately thought that if she'd wanted to go all girly, she should have had her long blond hair curled into ringlets instead of leaving it straight. Attention to detail was the keynote of a successful image. Mel was an expert at that.

'And you look absolutely divine in your pin-striped morning suit,' Vanessa tossed back at him.

Ah, the fun of flirting, Jake thought, but not nearly as much fun as the verbal duelling battles with Mel Rossi. He was going to miss them while she was away on vacation. The temporary assistant she had organised would not provide anything like the same stimulating challenges. All next month without Mel would be dead flat.

Vanessa did not give his mind any exercise. On the other hand, she certainly provided considerable physical exercise in bed, enjoying sex every bit as much as he did. Strait-laced Mel would probably only approve of the missionary position. Though sometimes when those golden-amber eyes of hers cast him a particularly sultry look, hot and heavy with suppressed passion, he wondered...

She'd given him that look just before he'd left work yesterday.

'Everything set for tomorrow?' he'd asked.

'If the plan you supplied of your grandfather's place is correct and the cake can be easily wheeled out to the rear terrace, the presentation should go without a hitch,'' she'd stated with confidence.

'That was a stiff fee for the woman you've hired,' he'd remarked—not criticising, just commenting, but it had raised Mel's hackles.

'She had to have fittings for the floral bikini, rehearsals to ensure the lift mechanism in the cake is worked properly and I didn't think your grandfather would appreciate anyone who came cheaply. I decided on quality.' Her eyebrows had arched in challenge. 'Do you have a problem with that, Jake?'

'Not if she's worth her hire.'

'Well, you can be the judge tomorrow.'

This final declaration had been accompanied by the sultry look—positively burning with passion. Maybe she *had* resented being given a task reeking of male chauvinism, and was making him pay for it in her own way. Not that he cared about the cost. Only the result mattered. And no doubt Mel's professionalism would produce the goods. Nevertheless, he now had a hot interest in the *quality* of the woman who emerged from the cake.

Red and white candy-striped umbrellas shaded the

tables set out on the back lawn for afternoon tea. It was a glorious day, the heat of the summer sun alleviated by a light cooling breeze from the harbour—perfect for sitting outside and enjoying the ambience.

White lace cloths adorned the round tables. Chairs upholstered in red surrounded them. Each place was set with a plate, cup and saucer in delicate bone china, accompanied by brilliantly polished silver cutlery and a starched white linen napkin in a silver holder.

When everyone was seated, the waiters served tea from elegant silver teapots and placed ornate five-tiered cakestands on the tables. From top to bottom, the tiers provided cucumber sandwiches, shortbread kisses, date scones, savoury puff pastries and a selection of rich cakes.

'This reminds me of High Tea at the Empress Hotel on Vancouver Island,' one of Jake's fellow guests at his table commented appreciatively, setting off comparisons with other grand hotels around the world.

From the happy buzz around the tables, it was obvious the party was a huge success. Speeches were merrily called for and merrily given. Jake waited until the final pièce de résistance—dishes of chocolate coated strawberries with clotted cream—had been served before excusing himself from the table and using his cell-phone to give the 'Go' command to the stage-hands whose job was to wheel in the birthday cake.

He quickly alerted the orchestra to start playing 'Happy Birthday' when the cake came to a halt, then moved to his grandfather's table where Byron Devila was playing host to his four daughters—by different wives—and their current spouses.

Jake's mother had long ago discarded his father, a

musician who'd been a mistake of her youth. Not that she
didn't still look youthful in her fifties. Her artfully blond
hair took years off her age and her relatively unlined face
was as pretty as ever. Amazing what cosmetic surgery and
almost unlimited funds could achieve.

'I've got a special surprise coming up for you, Pop,' Jake
announced.

'Splendid! I do love surprises!'

His grandfather was in fine form. No doubt he'd stirred
the jealousy pot amongst the four half sisters, mischievously pitting them against each other. He'd also done a
lot of table-hopping, spreading his charm around all the
female guests. Jake wondered if he'd already targeted his
next wife now that his seventh divorce had been finalised.

He was still a fine figure of a man. And handsome. His
flashing brown eyes had not lost their sparkle. The lines
on his well-tanned face—no age spots in evidence—were
mostly laughter lines and whatever sag he had around his
jaw was hidden by the neatly trimmed grey and black
beard. His nose retained its perky tilt and the moustache
beneath it accentuated the captivating sensuality of his
strongly carved mouth. Highly mobile black and grey
eyebrows made up for the fact he was almost bald.

Too much testosterone, Jake thought, and wondered if
his own hair would suffer the same fate as he grew older.
Not that it mattered, he decided. He liked to think he'd still
be sexually active when he was his grandfather's age.

'If you'll just turn your chair around to face the terrace,'
he instructed, 'your surprise is about to take centre stage.'

'Centre stage?' his grandfather mused as he rose to his
feet, eyes flashing with excited speculation. 'It's got to be
a troupe of dancing girls.'

'Oh, Dad!' his youngest daughter chided.

'He's never going to act his age,' an older one advised her.

'Why should he when he doesn't have to?' Jake's mother slid in, giving her father a sweetly indulgent smile, bolstering her *favourite daughter* status.

'Hey! Take a look at that!' one of the party guests called out in amazement.

All attention was immediately swung towards the terrace, zeroing in on the monster cake which was making its appearance stage right. It was being wheeled in from the wide garden path by four guys dressed in white with Happy Birthday, surrounded by the outline of a heart, printed in red on their T-shirts.

Nice touch, Mel, Jake thought, and took a mental note to compliment her on it when she came back to work.

His grandfather laughed and clapped Jake on the shoulder. 'You didn't!' he cried, his eyes dancing with the memory of his favourite movie.

'I did!' Jake answered with happy satisfaction in his grandfather's delight.

'Is she a match for Virna Lisi?'

'We'll see.'

'I'm bursting with anticipation.'

So am I, Jake thought. The cake was a masterpiece of decorative art—scrolls and flowers, probably made of plaster of Paris, edging the tiers, red satin ribbon tied in bows beneath them. The candles actually held electric globes and were alight, which meant power had to be supplied by a small generator inside the cake. Another brilliant idea by Mel! So far this production had definitely upstaged the movie.

'Eight tiers,' Jake pointed out. 'One for each decade of your life, Pop.'

'And the best is yet to come,' was the resounding reply.

Certainly a tribute to positive thinking! Jake hoped he'd feel the same way when he was eighty.

Grandfather and grandson stood side by side, watching the cake come to a halt. Once it was in position at the centre of the terrace, two of the stage-hands brought a roll of carpet from the back of the bottom tier.

'Lay it out, boys!' Byron called, happily stepping forward to meet the end of it.

Red carpet, of course! Another plus score for Mel's initiative. She deserved a bonus for this.

Fortunately the orchestra had the sense to hold off starting to play until the scene was completely set. Jake couldn't resist trailing his grandfather, standing just behind his shoulder to get a full frontal view of the *quality* woman Mel had hired. There was an excited buzz of anticipation from the party crowd behind them. Without a doubt, this act was going to be talked about for a long, long time. People actually gasped as the lid of the top tier slowly lifted back.

The orchestra swung into action, producing a rousing rendition of 'Happy Birthday.' Everyone sang enthusiastically. A blonde head started to emerge from the top of the cake—lustrous shiny hair in a soft, wavy Marilyn Monroe style, a flyaway fringe swept across the forehead. Her eyes were lowered, lids shaded in a smoke-grey, crescents of long dark lashes brushing her cheeks. A very sexy mouth was emphasised by glossy red lipstick.

It wasn't until her face and neck had completely emerged from the cake that recognition hit Jake and it came like a massive explosion inside his head.

Forget the deceptive blonde hair.

What he was looking at was *Mel Rossi's* face.

Unmistakable!

The shock of it totally rattled Jake's sense of reality. Never in a million years would he have imagined his prim and proper personal assistant taking on the role of blond bimbo in a birthday cake! It was completely beyond belief. Yet here she was, undeniably emerging, the lush curves of her body on stunning display.

The bikini she wore was fashioned out of red roses. They had to be artificial flowers but looked very real, and Jake's mind instantly conjured up a vision of *this* Mel artfully posed nude on a red satin sheet being showered by American Beauty rose petals. With himself doing the showering. It was a stimulating vision. A very arousing vision.

She even had a red satin heart-shaped cushion dangling from a red ribbon around her wrist. Jake's heart was not in such good shape. It was thumping wildly as his gaze followed Mel's slow elevation from the cake, right down to sexy, red, high heeled sandals on her feet.

'Wow!' his grandfather breathed on a sigh of sheer awe. 'You've outdone yourself, my boy!'

Jake was speechless.

He hadn't heard the birthday song end but it obviously had because people were applauding, men whistling, cries of 'Bravo!' rang in his ears. His mesmerised gaze travelled back up to Mel's face, just as she lifted her lashes.

And...*choong*!

Her eyes shot sizzling bolts of heat straight at him.

Nothing was suppressed in that look!

Even his toes curled.

Amid the chaos of the moment, some deeply intuitive sense in Jake Devila told him his relationship with Mel Rossi had just been changed...forever!

CHAPTER FOUR

A BLAZE of satisfaction settled Merlina's quivering nerves. Jake looked completely stunned. And he wasn't recovering quickly, either. Shock had blanked out the usual vitality of his playboy handsome face. There were no dimples in his cheeks. His mouth was absolutely still, not so much as a twitch of amusement. His dark eyes were not enlivened by mischievously teasing twinkles. He stared at her as though dazed. Mesmerised.

No doubt about it.

She had socked it to him with a vengeance.

And here she was, on show, in a bikini, and proud of herself for having dared to do it. A liberated woman. Her own person.

All the time and attention she had poured into producing this scenario had just paid off. She could retire from the battle scene of her employment with honours on her side. No sense of defeat at all!

But she still had to finish the act and do it absolutely right. She hoped all the rehearsals of stepping down the tiers of the cake in these sexy red shoes would stand her in good stead. Teetering would be terrible at this point. She fastened her gaze on Byron Devila, obviously the man standing at the end of the red carpet and just in front of Jake, then turned on a slow, sensual smile designed to warm the cockles of his eighty-year-old manhood.

Though he didn't look eighty, more like a young sixty, and the smile he returned smacked of very lively male appreciation of how she looked. Which gave Merlina the encouragement she needed to set off descending to the red carpet which led directly to him.

Think Marilyn Monroe, she told herself. The orchestra took it upon itself to play 'Some Enchanted Evening' as she made her way down the steps, for which Merlina was intensely grateful. It was much easier to look sexily graceful moving to music than in silence with everyone watching. She arrived on the red carpet without a falter, and determinedly ignoring Jake, she walked straight towards his grandfather, growing in delicious confidence with every step.

She'd done it and it was wonderful!

She felt Jake's gaze on her, felt a churning maelstrom of thoughts coming from him and swirling around her. Her nerves were very active again, not quivering with the fear of failure as before, but buzzing with elation at having thrown the puppet master into a wild tangle with his own strings.

And Byron Devila was looking at her as she'd always wished Jake would—with sparkling admiration and captivated interest. The triumph of it all was exhilarating. The smile on her face grew in brilliance. Her eyes danced with daredevil glee at the older man. He held out his hands in open welcome as her approach came to a halt. She unhooked the ribbon from her wrist and presented him with the red satin heart-shaped cushion.

'Happy Birthday, Mr Devila. May your heart always be filled with joy,' she said, beaming her own joy right at him.

'It is, my dear, and you've put it there.' He hooked the ribbon attached to the cushion around his own wrist, then took both her hands in his, pressing lightly, his eyes twinkling encouragement. 'I prefer at this point in my life not to waste any time. Tell me your name.'

'It's Merlina,' she replied with an arch emphasis for Jake's benefit. 'Merlina Rossi.'

'Merlina…' He rolled it off his tongue as though finding it much to his taste. 'A beautiful name for a beautiful woman.'

'Thank you, Mr Devila.'

'Call me Byron.'

'Thank you, Byron.'

'Now the only other question is—' he waggled his eyebrows in flirtatious appeal '—will you marry me?'

She laughed. Whether it was a joke or not, there was such delicious irony in being proposed to by the grandfather of the man she really wanted, right in front of him.

'That's going a bit far, Pop,' Jake said in an irritable tone, not the least bit amused. 'You've only just laid eyes on her.'

'Ah, yes! Love at first sight. Nothing like it!' Byron said with relish, his eyes not leaving hers for a second. 'Thank you for choosing Merlina for me, Jake.'

'I didn't choose her!' he rasped in exasperation. 'And you can't have her. She's mine!'

'Yours?' Byron turned a frown to his grandson. 'You've had a skinny model hanging off you all afternoon. Go back to her, my boy. You can't have it two ways, you know.'

Absolutely right, Merlina thought darkly, warming to Byron Devila who clearly understood how relationships should work. She gave Jake a look of hot scorn for his playboy ways. If he wanted her to be his, he was going to have to drop every other woman and fight his grandfather for her. Leap through a few of her hoops, too. Like marriage and children. Which wouldn't happen. She knew that. But it didn't extinguish the wild fantasy of a life-changing miracle suddenly happening.

'Mel happens to be my personal assistant!' Jake bit out menacingly.

'Mel? Mel? Who is Mel?' His grandfather demanded.

Merlina was beginning to love Byron Devila. He was fighting on her front, forcing Jake to acknowledge her real name.

'This woman you're so taken with is Mel,' came the belligerent reply. Jake waved his hand in a scissor-like movement that clearly wanted to cut this scene to its end immediately. He glared at Merlina to confirm his statement.

No way, she beamed back at him. *You can stew in this juice all by yourself. I'm not rescuing you. Not ever again.*

'You should be shot for corrupting such a beautiful name,' Byron declared, returning his attention to Merlina, smiling at her as though she was all the goodies in the world wrapped up in one package. 'It's the feminine version of Merlin, the great magician, and you hold me spellbound, my dear.'

Oh, he was good! This was real heady stuff! No wonder he'd wooed seven women into wedlock. His immense wealth might be one attraction but the man himself was an absolute charmer.

'Tell him!' Jake commanded, positively fizzing with frustration. 'Tell him you're my personal assistant.'

Merlina took a deep breath and sighed with blissful satisfaction in her erstwhile employer's disarray. 'I *was* Jake's personal assistant, Byron,' she said to her new admirer. 'But I'm not anymore.'

'What do you mean you're *not*?' Jake fumed.

She fluttered her eyelashes at him. 'I left my resignation on your desk yesterday afternoon. You no longer have any claim on my time, Jake.'

He was stunned again.

Temporarily speechless.

It was marvellous!

She smiled sweetly at his grandfather. 'So I'm free to spend as much time with you as I like, Byron.'

'Bravo!' he approved.

But Jake wasn't finished yet. He came back firing. 'You can't leave me without notice.' His eyes glittered satisfaction as he reminded her, 'It's not ethical, Mel.'

'I believe a month's notice is more than sufficient to fulfil my obligation to you, Jake. I mentioned it in my note of resignation. You have the next month to find my replacement.'

Realisation hit him, drawing his brows into a glowering frown. 'But you'll be away on vacation all that time.'

'Yes. And I am due that vacation, as you very well know.' *Not having had one in the nineteen months she'd been his slave!*

'Splendid!' Byron approved heartily. 'Where would you like to spend it, Merlina? Say the word and I'll...'

'Merlina...' Jake grated out between gnashing teeth, 'is not a true blonde.'

Had he burst a blood vessel?

To attack on such a personal level...

Byron rolled his eyes at him. 'Neither is your skinny model, my boy. Do be a good chap and go back to her. I understand your disappointment in losing Merlina to me but you obviously didn't appreciate her enough.'

Too true! she thought, definitely beginning to love Jake's grandfather.

'I'm not talking about bottle blondes,' came the fierce retort. 'Her hair is dark brown. She's wearing a wig!'

That was a mean blow. Completely below the belt.

Byron re-appraised her hair. 'Damned good wig!' he approved. 'Had me fooled.'

Jake went for the kill. 'And she's fooling with you, Pop.'

Byron grinned at her. 'Nothing like having a beautiful woman fooling with me.'

The tight place in Merlina's chest loosened up as imminent humiliation passed. She grinned back. 'I wore it to please you on your birthday, Byron. Jake said you preferred blondes.'

'Well, I now find myself leaning towards sassy brunettes. And speaking of my birthday...' Byron half turned, offering his arm to her. 'Allow me to escort you to my table where we can toast it together.'

'How kind!' she purred, curling her arm around his.

She wasn't sure if Jake actually growled but he looked at her as though he'd like to go for her throat. The aggression emanating from him was definitely dangerous. And thrilling.

Byron patted her hand and smiled benevolently at his grandson. 'Thank you, Jake. Best birthday gift you could have given me.' He blithely waved a dismissal. 'You can have the cake rolled away now but I'm keeping Merlina. And please ask the orchestra to play Lerner and Loewe's classic, 'The Night They Invented Champagne.'

Jake was left standing in fight mode with nothing to fight as Byron led Merlina away in a triumphant walk back towards his guests. *Maybe he'll kick the cake,* she thought, and decided to flirt outrageously with his grandfather for as long as the party lasted.

'Oh, what fun!' Byron burbled in her ear. 'I take it you have issues with my grandson and you've just given him a wake-up call.'

She smiled at him, noting the merry amusement in his eyes. 'Something like that.'

'Brilliantly done, my dear. Don't know what he sees in all those skinny women.'

She sighed. 'I don't think it will change anything, Byron.'

'Nonsense! You have him on toast.'

'Just the heat of the moment. And that does my pride a lot of good,' she wryly confessed. 'But unlike you, Jake isn't the marrying type, and I've already wasted too much of my life on him.'

'This is not the day to give up, Merlina. You're on the crest of a wave and you must ride it through,' he advised. 'It's time the boy did get married and I heartily approve of you as my granddaughter-in-law. A sassy woman puts a bit of excitement in one's life.'

She laughed, hugging his arm with real affection. 'You are a darling, Byron. But I don't think…'

'Leave it to me. I'm a master of manoeuvres.'

'I'd have to agree with that. Asking me to marry you was wonderful!'

'We can play on it. Give me the pleasure of your company and I'll give you a diamond engagement ring.'

Merlina halted, suddenly unsure of where she was going with Jake's grandfather. 'Byron, I think you're a lovely man but I couldn't really marry you.'

He laughed. 'Just setting the cat amongst the pigeons, my dear. How long did you work for Jake?'

'Nineteen months.'

'So the hook is well and truly in, even if he doesn't know it yet.'

Merlina shook her head. 'I wouldn't go that far. He's had a string of women while I've been working for him.'

Byron nodded knowingly. 'The best of both worlds without having to give any commitment.' He patted her hand again. 'Let's nail the pay-time. Be my live-in companion for a week. Just one more week of your life, Merlina, to see if Jake will come to your party.'

It was a tempting prospect. The idea of driving Jake Devila into a jealous rage was the stuff of giddy dreams. If it could actually happen…

'I promise you we'll have fun. I'll take you shopping. Trips to the theatre, dining out. I'll parade you everywhere, make us a conspicuous couple. I bet Jake won't be able to ignore that.'

'You're as much a devil as he is, Byron,' she said, thinking *Why not? A week of being a pampered companion would be easy to take, wouldn't it? Some fun time before looking for another job. And if her being with his grandfather did get to Jake…*

'Got his genes from me.'

Warning bells instantly rang. Byron Devila might be eighty but Merlina suspected he hadn't lost any of his virility. She drilled him with her eyes. 'I'd need you to be an absolute gentleman if I'm to live in.'

He laughed. 'Hands off, I promise. I know where your interest lies, Merlina, and I'm feeling very inclined to further it if I can.'

She believed him. With a mad sense of throwing her hat well and truly over the windmill, she said, 'Okay. I'll do it.'

'That's my girl!' he rolled out with beaming approval. 'What a lovely birthday I'm having. Now let me introduce you to Jake's mother.'

And they resumed their stroll towards his table.

Behind them the orchestra started to play 'The Night They Invented Champagne.'

CHAPTER FIVE

JAKE returned to his table, furiously smouldering over Mel's—*Merlina's*—hijack of his birthday surprise. It made his grandfather's delight in her totally intolerable. She'd done it to thumb her nose at his male chauvinist game, to put the icing on the cake of her resignation, to walk away wagging her rose petalled bottom at him. He was so burned up by her triumphant exit from his life, he could barely respond to the bubbling good humour of his friends, the guys in particular.

'Got to hand it to you, Jake. That was a maxi show-stopper. Marilyn Monroe and *American Beauty* rolled out in one!'

'Top wow factor. Talk about sex on legs!'

'If *she* was in the garden, any man might be tempted to take time out to smell the roses!'

'Looks like your grandfather is doing just that. Good one, Jake!'

'Where did you find her?'

'I bet she cost a bomb.'

A bomb that had exploded right in his face. And the cost was totally unacceptable. Losing Mel as his personal assistant...there was going to be one hell of a hole in his life. Then he remembered the exorbitant fee for *the model*. That was a kiss-my-arse hit if ever there was one. He almost erupted as he thought of how Mel had fooled him and feather-bedded her retirement from the job.

'I was not counting the cost,' he replied, using every gram of control not to sound as violently put out as he felt. 'I just wanted to please my grandfather.' *And get under Mel's skin.* Except she'd got under his instead. Big time!

'No doubt about that,' Vanessa said dryly, nodding towards his grandfather's table. 'He's obviously smitten with her.'

There he was, introducing Mel to his mother and aunts and she was laughing her head off. Jake's hands curled into fists. Then, to really rub salt into his wound, one of the guys commented, 'Definitely worth every cent she cost. Where did you say you found her, Jake?'

'Oh, really!' Vanessa interjected, a jealous note creeping in. 'All this leching over the star turn is a bit rude in front of the women at this table.'

Female agreement swiftly followed, though in a more good-humoured tone than Vanessa's waspish scolding. Which reminded him that his grandfather had always said skinny women thought too much of themselves. It had probably put Vanessa's nose out of joint to be upstaged by a woman with a far more voluptuous figure.

Jake tried to give her the attention she wanted, but his heart wasn't it. He didn't even find her attractive any more. As for having sex with her tonight…no, he didn't want to. In fact, he could barely resist the magnetic pull of following Mel's progress with his grandfather.

No way would he give his erstwhile personal assistant more satisfaction by showing an interest in her outrageous gallivanting at this party, but it was damned difficult to keep his gaze trained on Vanessa and his other companions, and he found the popping of champagne corks a major irritation. The whole situation turned into an agony of waiting for the party to end.

Eventually guests started leaving. His friends decided on continuing the evening at a fashionable bar. Jake didn't want to accompany them. He was in no mood to be civil let alone convivial. Vanessa was seriously put out when he excused himself, inventing some other commitment. He suggested she go with the others if she was so inclined and she rather sulkily said she would.

It made Jake wonder how he could have ever thought she was desirable on any level. Nevertheless, pride insisted he didn't end their relationship while Mel could still see them together. To his over-burdened mind, that would give the highly provocative Ms Rossi not only the icing on the cake, but the cake, too.

She was hooked to his grandfather's arm, saying goodbye to guests, playing hostess to his host with all the aplomb of a seasoned performer, which irked Jake to the bone. He put his left arm around Vanessa's waist as they approached to take their leave.

'Great party, Pop,' he said, showing as much teeth as was possible to put into a broad smile.

His grandfather shot out his right hand to give Jake's a strong shake. 'Made more so by you, my boy. Can't thank you enough.'

'Yes, the cake idea was brilliant,' Merlina trilled happily. 'I've had such a wonderful time with Byron.'

Jake steeled himself to look at her. 'Thank you,' he said, grimly holding his smile. 'And may I compliment you on once again rising to the occasion.' Then to underline how gracious he could be in defeat and to minimise his previous bad-tempered reaction, he added, 'I wish you well in whatever occupation you choose next, Mel.' *Be damned if he'd call her Merlina!*

'Which will be married life if I have anything to do with it,' his grandfather supplied, twinkling indulgently at her.

'Oh, Byron!' she purred, hugging his arm in demonstrative pleasure.

Jake felt his innards being clawed.

The lion in him came roaring out, wanting to carry Mel Rossi off and do some clawing of his own.

'Do you have transport home?' he asked, trying his utmost to sound considerate and caring.

She smiled, the golden amber eyes glowing warmly. 'How kind! But I don't need transport. Byron has asked me to stay here with him and I am so enjoying his company…'

'What about clothes?' came straight out of his mouth. The image of her prancing around in her rose bikini throughout a private evening with his grandfather made him want to club her over the head and drag her off to a cave.

'I brought a change of clothes with me,' she answered with limpid ease. 'The butler kindly agreed to mind my bag until the party was over. You don't have to worry about me, Jake.'

'No, I'm sure he doesn't,' Vanessa slid in snidely. 'Thank you for a lovely party, Byron.'

'Glad you enjoyed yourself, my dear,' he replied, brimming over with enough bonhomie to indulgently encompass a skinny woman who was showing signs of becoming bitchy.

'Take care, Pop,' Jake managed to toss out before leading Vanessa away.

'I'm going to take care of Merlina instead,' his grandfather declared extravagantly. 'We're off shopping tomorrow.' He grinned at her in delighted anticipation. 'There are some splendid boutiques in Double Bay. And we can have a marvellous seafood lunch at Doyle's. The maître d' can always find a table for me.'

'Oh, goody!' the femme fatale cried, snuggling closer to her sugar daddy.

Enough was more than enough!

Jake departed in a simmering rage, dragging Vanessa along with him. 'Don't walk so fast,' she protested. 'I'm wearing very high heels, you know.'

'You can be barefoot in the park for all I care,' he growled, having completely lost any semblance of playboy charm.

Vanessa came to a dead halt, spitting mad. 'You had her lined up for yourself, didn't you?'

The accusation pulled Jake up, too. 'No, I didn't,' he bit out.

'You hung around her after she came out of the cake and a moment ago you wanted to take her home,' came the peevish argument. 'What's more, you're now in a pet because she prefers to be with Byron.'

'*In a pet*?' Jake repeated incredulously.

'Don't bother denying it! And don't think I'm going to play second fiddle to a birthday cake bimbo. Goodbye, Jake! I'll leave with Tim and Fiona.'

Having slapped him with *her* rejection, she turned her back on him, strutted several haughty paces, then half-turned to hurl a piece of spite at him. 'I hope she becomes your step-grandmother!'

Over my dead body!

Jake stood stock-still as the thought crashed through his mind with stunning violence.

For once in his life he didn't know what to do.

He didn't have a plan.

Running after Vanessa made no sense. He didn't want to hang onto her. Best that their relationship be severed and it didn't matter who'd done the severing. Let Vanessa have the satisfaction of being the one to walk away.

But Mel Rossi's defection was something else.

That was definitely a blow below the belt.

He had to fight back.

He had to win.

She was using his grandfather as a weapon and a shield but once she was on her own…

Tonight, when she returned to her apartment at Chatswood, he'd be waiting for her, and no way was he about to let Mel Rossi close her door on him!

Midnight…and she hadn't come home!

Jake's frustration knew no bounds. She had to be staying overnight at the Vaucluse mansion. In any event, there was no point in camping here any longer. Even if she turned up now, he'd look like a jealous fool for waiting to confront her at this hour, and he was not—*not*—a jealous fool. He knew what she was up to, playing a one-upmanship end-game, and if nothing else, he was determined to get in the last word.

He drove home to Milson's Point with that resolution burning in his mind.

However, opening up the opportunity to get in the last word proved difficult. Mel did not answer her telephone on Sunday and Jake seethed over the possibility that she was, indeed, out shopping and lunching with his grandfather. He told himself to calm down. It was only a matter of waiting out some more time before he caught up with her.

Monday was filled with more frustration. He found it increasingly wearing to be civil to his temporary assistant because she wasn't Mel. She was a skinny blonde who kept transmitting availability signals which sparked no interest whatsoever. In fact, he suspected Mel had gone out of her way to find a woman who fitted the type he usually dated. Another slap in the face!

And still he was only getting the answering machine when he telephoned her apartment. Had she already left on her vacation? *Or*…no, it was beyond belief that she really was cosying up to his grandfather. That had only been a game…hadn't it?

He called the Vaucluse mansion.

The butler answered.

'It's Jake,' he said quickly. 'Is my grandfather in, Harold?'

'Mr Byron is out today.'

Jake hesitated, but the need to know drove the question. 'What about Ms Rossi?'

'Ms Rossi accompanied Mr Byron.'

Jake's stomach clenched. 'When will they be home?' shot out of his mouth.

'Dinner is to be served at the usual hour so I'm expecting them to return before then.'

Them! Not just his grandfather!

Jake forced himself to say, 'Thank you, Harold. I'll call later.'

'Any message, sir?'

'No. Thank you.'

It was impossible to apply himself to any work. His mind kept churning over the situation with Mel. Was it going beyond a game? His grandfather had the wealth to wrap a woman in however much luxury she desired but surely Mel wouldn't consider marrying an eighty-year-old man.

Maybe she'd taken up the position of *his* personal assistant, with the promise of lots of perks on the side. His grandfather would spoil her rotten and enjoy every minute of doing it. And Mel would perform brilliantly as she always did.

Damn them both!

That scenario was almost as hard to swallow as marriage. But what could he do about it? He chewed over the problem and was still chewing it over when his temporary assistant alerted him to a call from Vanessa Hall. With considerable effort he reset his mind to dealing with the other fallout from his grandfather's party. It was now late afternoon and he hoped she didn't want to press for a reconciliation.

'Vanessa…what can I do for you?' he asked blandly.

'I've just come home from doing a charity luncheon fashion parade…'

Reminding him she was a queen of the catwalk and should be valued accordingly.

'Guess who was there, Jake,' she prompted silkily.

His spine crawled. 'Do tell,' he drawled, knowing instantly what this call was about and resolving to sound uncaring.

'Byron and your cake bimbo,' she crowed.

'No doubt they were enjoying themselves.'

'Oh, yes! The champagne was flowing. For good reason. She's now wearing a huge, flashy, diamond solitaire ring on her engagement finger. Happy days, Jake! You might get to kiss the bride.'

CHAPTER SIX

MERLINA was beginning to appreciate how very seductive the lifestyle of the mega-wealthy could be. The bedroom suite she was currently occupying was absolute luxury, and from the moment she'd stepped into Byron's amazing mansion, she hadn't done a single chore—no cooking, no cleaning, no washing, ironing or tidying up. Her only job was to look good and be ready to do whatever Byron decided they should, which invariably involved the pursuit of pleasure in one form or another.

In a purely pampering sense, this was the best start to a vacation she'd ever had, though it was impossible not to think about Jake and how her departure from his life might be affecting him. Had he missed her at work today? Or was the new temporary assistant—chosen in a fit of female pique—providing the kind of distraction a playboy appreciated?

She glanced down at the magnificent diamond ring Byron had insisted she wear, arguing that it was a necessary prod to produce results. Her fingers automatically wriggled to catch the light in the facets of the fabulous gem. It was seductive, too, but not all the wealth in the world could give her what she really wanted. Could this pretend engagement to his grandfather pry Jake from his free-wheeling life-style?

With a heavy sigh, she picked up her hairbrush, determined on not letting the answer to that nagging question mean too much to her. She had a life to live no matter what, and right now it was better to concentrate on presenting a picture of perfect grooming for Byron.

While the blond wig had worked effectively at the birthday party, she much preferred her own natural dark brown hair for real life and wasn't about to change it. If Jake didn't find her so desirable as a brunette, that was his problem, not hers. Such a superficial thing should be irrelevant. It was the person to person attraction that put depth into a relationship—enough depth for a marriage to work.

Having refreshed her make-up, Merlina checked her overall appearance in the cheval mirror before going downstairs for pre-dinner drinks with Byron. She was wearing one of her new dresses from yesterday's shopping spree—a tan and white polka dot silk wrap-around with a wide tan leather belt cinching in her waist. It was both elegant and sexy and she loved it, especially teamed with the new Ferragamo tan and white shoes. A classy outfit for job interviews, she'd decided, and didn't care how much it had cost.

If Jake did not *rise to the occasion*, she was determined to start afresh, setting aside everything linked to him, including the type of clothes she'd chosen to fit into the company image. Stodgy black suits were out, too. They'd been a hangover from what her family had expected of her, and coincidentally suitable for her previous job since her Queen Bee magazine boss had hated anyone stealing her limelight. Now she had the confidence to create her own style and stick to what she liked for herself.

It was also time she found a husband, though where she was going to find a man she'd want to spend her life with was definitely a problem. After being with Jake...she shook her head. Making comparisons was stupid. Besides, hadn't she thought all along that Jake wasn't marriage material?

Though Byron thought he might be, given enough provocation to realise that she was *the one* for him to marry. The hope that her benevolent match-maker's reading of the situation was right kept pumping through her heart. Dreams did not die easily.

But whatever the outcome of Byron's manoeuvres, she still had to look for a new position. There was no going back to what had been. Moving forward, one way or another, was the only option.

Having set her mind straight once again, Merlina went downstairs to the main reception room. As she entered it, she couldn't help thinking that only the mega-wealthy would choose white sofas. They looked wonderfully dramatic set amongst beautifully polished antique furniture and the gloriously coloured rugs on the parquet floor, but they'd be hell to keep clean in any normal living area.

Byron, looking sartorially splendid in white trousers and shirt, teamed with a beige linen jacket, swung around from a cocktail cabinet from which he'd just collected two crystal flute glasses. He beamed at her at her as though she was the best plaything he'd ever picked up. No doubt about it. Jake took after his grandfather.

'Good news, my dear!' he cried triumphantly. 'Harold has just informed me that Jake called this afternoon and he asked about *you*!'

Her pulse skipped haphazardly at this evidence that Jake hadn't simply wiped her out of his life as she'd thought he might, his ego smarting at her bold and abrupt departure from the place he'd put her in.

'It could just be a problem at work,' common sense forced her to say.

Byron grinned at her. 'He also asked when would we be home? I am confidently anticipating a visit from him this evening.'

'He probably asked out of irritation that I wasn't readily available,' Merlina muttered.

'Oh, ye of little faith,' Byron mocked good-humouredly, his eyes twinkling devilment. 'You're forgetting our trump card.'

'The engagement ring? But how could he know so soon?'

'I'm betting that Vanessa Hall couldn't wait to tell him.'

'Why would she?'

'Because she had her nose royally out of joint when Jake showed too much interest in you on Saturday. Trust me. I know women.'

Merlina couldn't argue with that. Byron had married seven of them and no doubt had experience of many more. He oozed gleeful confidence as he strolled forward to place a glass of champagne in her hand and click his own glass against hers.

'To success, my dear.'

Counting chickens before they hatched was not a good idea, Merlina reminded herself. Nevertheless, Byron's toast was irresistible. She did hope for success, though she couldn't feel the same confidence he did. They were both sipping the champagne when the butler made an entrance.

'Yes, Harold?' Byron invited.

'I've just opened the security gates for Mr Jake, sir.'

'Splendid! Right on cue!'

A host of butterflies invaded Merlina's stomach.

The butler, a tall, thin man in his fifties, very conscious of his dignity, unbent enough to smile at his employer's pleasure. 'Will it be three for dinner, sir?'

'I doubt my grandson will be in the mood to dine with us tonight. Hold dinner back until I give the word, Harold.'

'As you wish, sir.'

Door chimes called Harold out of the room to greet their visitor and let him in.

'That was quick,' Byron commented with amusement. 'Jake must have burned up the driveway. Are you primed for confrontation, Merlina?'

She took a deep breath, trying to calm herself. This was it—the moment of truth! Jake's reaction to the situation would tell her if she meant anything to him beyond a wound to his ego.

'The game is on,' she said with gritty determination.

Hearty approval smiled back at her. 'That's my girl!'

It brought a smile to her face. If Jake's grandfather ended up accomplishing nothing else with this marriage campaign, he had certainly done *her* ego a lot of good, making her feel like a woman worth having.

'Now drink up,' he instructed. 'We're celebrating, remember? Besides which, the champagne will put some fizz in your brain.'

'Right!' she agreed, and gulped down some of the heady liquor.

But the fizz came with Jake's entrance and it was electric, charging through every cell in Merlina's body.

'I hear congratulations are in order,' came the mocking drawl.

Her heart leapt. Pins and needles attacked her skin.

Merlina barely stopped herself from spinning around to face him. She had to hold on to control. It was the only way to deal with Jake.

'You hear right, my boy,' Byron answered with great aplomb, giving her a moment to collect herself.

She pasted a smile on her face and turned, lifting her left hand to show off the highly ostentatious ring. 'We're engaged to be married,' she lilted happily.

Jake's thin-lipped smile did not project any happiness for her. It didn't even put the usual dimples in his cheeks. There was a killer look in the dark brown eyes as they raked her from head to foot, ignoring the brilliant diamond ring they were supposed to fix on. He wore the usual casual jeans and T-shirt he favoured for work but there was nothing casual about the tension emanating from him, putting her nerves on edge.

'How fortunate! You won't have to look for another job,' he said with the silky cut of a stiletto to the heart.

The implication that she had leapt onto a free ride with his grandfather brought a rush of scorching heat to her face. She was no gold-digger and hated to be viewed as such. Yet reason told her Jake could hardly view her as anything else in the circumstances and it was impossible to protest. The sting would go right out of the game if she told the truth.

Byron laughed, rescuing her from the miserable moment. 'I think Merlina will have her work cut out handling the role of my wife. I can see us leading a very busy life. A long, lei- surely trip around the world to begin with…'

'Yes. Her planning is impeccable,' Jake sliced in. 'An attribute I've sorely missed today. Her temporary replace- ment is a featherbrain. If you don't mind, Pop, I'd like a private word with Mel. Hopefully it might sort out the mess her leaving has caused.'

Work!

He didn't care about her life.

He only cared about his precious business.

'That's up to Merlina,' Byron corrected him. 'And might I add you're really stretching her good nature by calling her Mel. She's always hated it, you know. Not wise diplomacy if you want her to help you.'

'You're right.' He sketched a half-bow to Merlina. 'I apologise for tampering with your name once again. Bad habit.' His eyes glittered more of a demand than an appeal as he added, 'If you'll just oblige me on this matter…'

'Yes, yes,' she said with a spurt of impatience, her conscience pricking her over having left him with problems. 'I'm sorry about the replacement. I thought you'd like her.'

His jaw tightened as though she'd hit him. And so she had. The deliberate choice of a skinny blonde to be her replacement had been intended as a slap in the face. Pure spite on her behalf, having felt diminished by the choices he'd made in the women who shared his private life. But business was business and she shouldn't have let personal issues sway her judgement.

'Well, I'll leave the two of you to sort things out,' Byron said benevolently. 'Would you like to join us for dinner, my boy? Lift a glass to our future?'

'No, thank you,' came the curt reply, tempered quickly by another thin-lipped smile. 'Your gain is my loss. I don't feel like drinking to it tonight.'

Byron nodded. 'Understood. Another time. I'll go and tell Harold you won't be staying.'

Merlina felt the tension in the room move up several

notches as Byron left it, closing the door behind him. She stared down at what was left of the champagne in her glass, wishing it could drown the dreadful sense of disappointment tearing at her heart. The game seemed very silly now. Like chasing pie in the sky. Nevertheless, she wasn't about to confess the truth to Jake. Pride insisted that she hold the line.

'I see you've already changed your image, dressing to suit my grandfather's life-style.'

The biting cynicism in his voice jerked her chin up. Anger flared. 'I'm dressed to suit myself, Jake. This is me. I'm done with fitting into an image. I'm not your...your *front* girl any more. Your grandfather wasn't the only one who had a birthday last week. I did, too, not that it would mean anything to you, but it does to me. I'm thirty years old, not a trendy teenager.'

She banged her glass down on the table which served the white sofas and planted her hands on her hips in an aggressive flaunting of her preferred style. 'What's more, your grandfather likes me as I am. He approves of everything about me, dark hair and all!'

Jake's arm whipped up, stabbing a finger at her. 'I never asked you to change the colour of your hair.'

'No. Only to cut off what I'd been growing for years. Long hair has always been traditional in my family, but you didn't bother asking if I minded having it cut. It was your way or no way.'

'You could have told me. We were in negotiation.'

'I was fool enough to want the job.'

'Fool enough!' Outrage poured from him. 'It was the perfect job for you. You revelled in it. And I paid you top dollar. Not to mention the bonus you gave yourself for coming out of the cake.'

'I was worth every cent of it. You got precisely what you wanted for your money, Jake Devila.'

'No, I didn't!' His arms cut the air like scissors, emphatically demonstrating his frustration and dismissing her claim.

'So where did I fail you?' she shot back at him.

His mouth clamped into a grim angry line. His eyes glared black fury at her. His chest rose and fell with a swift intake and expulsion of air. He threw up his hands in an exasperated manner as he finally admitted, 'You didn't fail me. I need you back at work.'

The crux of the matter.

Jake was put out.

Merlina folded her arms across her chest in decisive determination to ward off any appeal he might make. Enough was enough. She was not going back. She was moving on.

'You managed before me. You'll manage after me,' she stated with cold precision.

'I don't want to,' he almost yelled at her. 'What will it take to get you back?'

'There's nothing you can offer me that will change my mind.'

His hands clenched into fists at his sides. He looked as if he'd like to strangle her. Obviously the violent energy storming through him needed some outlet. He broke into an angry pacing back and forth across the room.

Merlina remained absolutely still, viewing him with immense satisfaction. How many times had she wanted to strangle him? It was good to have the boot on the other foot for once, good to see him not in control of the situation. The guilt over her choice of a temporary replacement was gone.

Jake Devila deserved a bit of heartburn. He'd given her plenty.

'You can't marry my grandfather,' he fired at her, pulling up to deliver the shot, eyes boring into hers with blazing intensity.

It stirred a mountain of belligerence. 'Oh, yes I can!'

He shook his head in agitated negation. 'How can you bring yourself to marry such an old man?'

'I find Byron very young at heart.'

'He has an eighty-year-old body,' was sliced back at her with venom.

'Which he keeps very fit,' she answered with lofty disdain for his emphasis on the physical.

'That doesn't make it sexy,' he argued fiercely.

'Your grandfather is every bit as sexy as Sean Connery, who even at his age is regularly voted one of the sexiest film stars in the world. He has exactly the same twinkling brown eyes, the same charm of manner, the same charismatic presence…'

'So you're happy to go to bed with him, are you? A man old enough to be your grandfather?'

It did sound *off*, but Merlina was on a roll and she wasn't about to give Jake the satisfaction of winning any round of this game. 'Why not? Byron makes everything a pleasure and he knows what a woman wants.'

Jake's eyes suddenly narrowed, dangerous sparks shooting out of them as he started strolling towards her. 'And maybe you don't know any better. Is that it, *Merlina*? You've always been a good Italian girl?'

Her arms tightened across her chest as she started to quake inside. Jake was coming at her as though he meant to test her sexual experience. She was torn by the desire to know what it would be like with him even as a bitter pride insisted he'd be just feeding his male ego if she allowed him any intimate access to her.

'That's none of your business,' she snapped.

His mouth curled into a smile of sensual promise. 'I have a mind to make it my business.'

Her head started whirling as he closed in on her. She was so terribly vulnerable to the physical attraction he exerted. If he touched her, kissed her… 'Stop right there, Jake Devila!'

Her voice sounded shrill, defensive, fearful.

He stopped barely an arm's length away from her. 'Come on, Mel,' he purred seductively. 'You know it's always been there, sizzling between us.'

'My name is Merlina.'

He ignored the frantic protest, his eyes searing hers, demanding the truth. 'It was exciting, wasn't it? The way we sparred—punch and counter-punch, me throwing out the challenge, you meeting it, nailing it…'

Yes, it was. But… 'You're a playboy, Jake. I'm a thirty-year-old woman. I want to get married.'

'What for? Security? That's so boring. What you need and want is…'

'I want to have a family.' And she definitely didn't want to hear about the needs he might fulfil. That would only be a temporary thing with Jake, anyway. It wouldn't mean anything. If she gave into temptation she would just be another notch on his bedpost.

'You want children with my grandfather?' he retorted incredulously.

'Charlie Chaplin was still fathering children through his eighties,' she argued heatedly. 'And Byron has great genes to pass on. Look at you.'

'What about me?'

'You're smart, creative, good-looking. I'll have wonderful children with Byron.'

'You could have wonderful children with me,' he swiftly countered, briefly taking the wind out of her sails.

She came back, blowing hard. 'But you don't want them.'

'Who said I don't want them?'

'Do you?'

The direct challenge caught him out. 'I haven't thought about it.'

'Right!' she mocked savagely.

'That doesn't mean I can't think about it.'

'For how many years?'

He floundered and she went for the killer-strike, the bottom line. 'I want to start a family soon, Jake. You're a playboy who'll only waste my time. So get out of my life and stay out.'

'Leaving you to my grandfather?' The expression on his face underwent a violent change. The moment of uncertainty was swallowed up by impassioned determination. 'Like hell I will!' he growled, reaching for her, hauling her into his embrace, his eyes glittering with a wild recklessness. 'No way are you going to be his bride! You're mine, Merlina Rossi! *All* mine!'

CHAPTER SEVEN

MERLINA was so stunned by the raw possessiveness in Jake's voice and the sudden impact of being arm-locked against his hard muscular body, she didn't do or say anything to stop his mouth from crashing down on hers, taking instant advantage of the gasp that had left her lips parted, his tongue invading, teasing, goading her into response, twining with hers, activating an intense flood of excitement.

Sensation exploded through her, blowing all reason from her mind, creating chaos everywhere it went, making her heart gallop, her lungs scream for air, her stomach quiver, her thighs quake. Control over anything was completely lost. Her arms struggled out of their fold to wind around his neck, spurred on by her own need to possess, to hold onto this intimate connection with him.

She kissed him back as avidly as he kissed her, again and again and again in a rampant desire to feel his lust for her, the sheer blitzing power of it, the wild urgency of it engulfing her as his arms tightened their hold, pressing her so close her breasts were almost flattened against his chest. She revelled in feeling the strong drumming of his heart, the tense muscles in his thighs, the hard roll of his erection making its indentation on her soft flesh.

He wanted her.

That intoxicating knowledge blotted out every bit of common sense she'd tried to cling to and turned her into a woman who craved every part of this man. His hands slid down her back, curling around her bottom, lifting her into a more erotic fit with his body, and she willingly, wantonly rubbed herself against him, surrendering to the primitive urge to excite the same feverish excitement coursing through her, to incite him into taking what she was dying to give.

Time and place meant nothing.

Pride was forgotten.

The need to satisfy all the secret yearnings she'd tried to argue away was overwhelming.

'A-hem!'

The loud clearing of a throat seemed to come from a distance, an alien sound breaking into what should have remained intensely private, jolting the glorious flow of feeling. Jake reacted to it before she did, lifting his head and quickly tucking hers into the curve of his neck and shoulder, holding her protectively as he turned his face towards the intrusion.

'Please excuse me, sir…'

Harold's stiffly dignified voice penetrated the cocoon of Merlina's whirling inner world and cleared some of the dizzy fog in her brain. Even as the realisation of what she'd been doing slid into it, making her acutely conscious of where she was and who she was with, she felt Jake's chest heave for breath and a wave of tension made her stomach contract.

What would he say?

How would he explain this?

'Mr Byron is in the library,' Harold announced with amazing sang-froid. 'He was wondering how long this...ah...tête-à-tête is going to take?'

'Just a bit longer, Harold,' Jake answered in a harsh rasp. He swallowed hard then produced a smoother tone. 'Please inform my grandfather we will join him in the library very shortly.'

We will?

What for?

Having hopelessly compromised her dismissive stance with Jake by succumbing to a reckless disregard of realities, Merlina tried desperately to collect her wits before having to face up to the man who was still intent on not relinquishing his hold on her. She couldn't find the strength or will to break free of him. In any event, it was utterly untenable to put on an act of shocked outrage at the liberty he had taken with her when she had responded so unmistakably. So positively.

'Very well, sir,' Harold solemnly intoned and the click of the door being shut signalled his exit.

Jake inhaled even more deeply than before, then released his hand clamp on her head, dragging his fingers softly through her hair as he breathed out her name. 'Merlina?'

Her real name.

Hearing it spoken by him in such a caring tone made her heart lurch.

She wanted him to say more, to tell her he was as shaken as she was by the force of the passion that had swept away any rational thought. But the gentle tug on her hair meant he wanted her to lift her head and look at him. Dragging in a deep breath of her own to feed much-needed oxygen into her brain, she obliged him, realising that to see would probably be more telling than to hear.

There was no amusement in his eyes. No spark of triumph. His face was deadly serious and his gaze locked onto hers with a magnetic intensity that made any evasion impossible. 'I want you. You want me,' he stated unequivocally, then punched home his point. 'You can't marry my grandfather.'

There was no denying the wanting. And she hadn't intended marrying Byron, anyway. Where this was leading with Jake she didn't know. Maybe nowhere. But what had just happened made hanging on to the pretend engagement impossible. The game was over, regardless of what the final outcome might be.

'You're right,' she sighed. 'I can't marry your grandfather.'

'Good!' The word was loaded with relief and satisfaction. 'I'm glad we've got that settled.'

The fact that he was focussing on breaking her relationship with Byron felt wrong to Merlina. Yet wasn't it what he had come to accomplish? The real truth burst through the seductive possessiveness which had drawn her into surrendering to his will. Jake simply wanted her free of other commitments so he could play with her.

'But I'm not coming back to work with you,' she flung out emphatically, her eyes challenging any ownership he thought he'd secured.

'We'll talk about that later,' he said brushing her off. 'Right now we should go to the library and break the news. The sooner it's done, the better.'

He had her hugged to his side and walking her to the door before Merlina's mind caught up with processing his intention. She stopped dead, not sure how the scene would play out in the library. She and Byron had an understanding and she wanted to talk to him alone.

'No! You're not to do that,' shot straight out of her mouth.

Jake frowned at her belligerent resistance. 'Do what?'

'I'll tell Byron myself.'

'You need me in support,' he insisted, not liking the idea of her separating herself from him.

Was he worried she might change her mind?

Rattling his confidence seemed like a very good idea to Merlina. Jake Devila was altogether too fond of getting his own way. She was not about to let him direct her life again. As far as she was concerned the rules of their relationship had changed.

'It's cowardly to lean on someone else when the message to be delivered is so personal,' she argued. 'It's up to me to tell him. You would only aggravate the situation, Jake.'

'But I'm part of it.'

'Only in so far as you showed me I hadn't given enough weight to one of the factors in my planning,' she said as archly as she could, hoping to downplay the treacherous depth of her feelings for him.

He was shocked. 'You were using me as a measure?'

'Wasn't that your intention?'

'No…yes…no…' He shook his head in angry confusion. 'I did what I've wanted to do for a long time.' His eyes blazed with absolute certainty. 'And don't tell me you didn't want it, too!'

'A case of having my curiosity satisfied, Jake. Thank you for the experience. Now if you'll excuse me, Byron is waiting.'

The verbal exchange had diverted his attention from keeping her strongly secured at his side. She had pushed out of his hold and was heading for the door before he recollected himself to produce another pitch.

'You can't go on staying here, Merlina. It would be rubbing salt into the wound. I'll wait and drive you home after you've spoken to my grandfather.'

Byron would not be wounded. He was far more likely to be elated at having manipulated his grandson into open action and impatient for a report on how well his tactics had succeeded.

However, the resolute purpose in Jake's voice made her pause. Did he really want to be with her or was this all about winning? It was true that the natural progression from breaking the engagement would be to leave Byron's home, but that was really irrelevant. She needed to know how much Jake cared about her.

She glanced back, her heart pounding with the hope of seeing something other than a determination to get his own way on his face.

'Harold will organise someone to pack your things and load them in the car,' he went on, alpha male taking charge, expecting her to fall in with him.

'I can call a taxi,' she said, flouting his arrangements, trying to probe his feelings.

'No.' His eyes glittered with battle-readiness, warning her he'd take the fight to any ground she stood on. 'You're coming with me, Merlina.'

She instinctively defied his power to beat her into submission, her chin lifting in rebellion. 'Why should I?'

He gave her an all encompassing look that forcefully conjured up the intimate knowledge she'd given him, his gaze travelling over her curves, making her flesh prickle and heat at the mutual memory of how completely she had abandoned herself to the desire he had stoked with his kisses.

'Because we have unfinished business together,' he said, silkily evoking the prospect of complete sexual satisfaction.

Merlina shivered, knowing if she let him take her home, he'd expect to go to bed with her. The choice was hers right now.

Unfinished business...

There was a terrible truth in those words. A terribly seductive truth. She wanted this man, more deeply than she'd ever wanted any other, and the primitive tug to take what he was offering before she moved on, eroded the reasoning that it would just be another brief affair in his playboy life.

She would be hurt when he finished it, as he undoubtedly would when his pleasure in her waned, but at least she wouldn't die regretting not having had this experience with him. On the other hand, submission did not sit well with her. Let Jake sweat on her decision! It would be good to know how strong his desire for her was.

'Do what you like,' she tossed at him, as though she didn't care. 'I have to go and tell Byron I can't marry him.'

Jake watched her stiff-backed exit, barely controlling the cave-man urge to catch her, throw her over his shoulder and carry her off to his car. Merlina Rossi hadn't just burrowed under his skin. She was tearing at his guts. And not conceding him anything, despite the fact she had definitely—*definitely*—been his for the taking a few minutes ago. If Harold hadn't come in...

But now she'd retreated to their old battle-ground, meeting his challenge and dumping it back in his lap. Though at least he'd won something from her. The intolerable engagement with his grandfather was over. He'd blown that perverted little enterprise apart. It was just as well Harold had come in and caught them at it. Harold was an unimpeachable witness. No way could Merlina make out she hadn't been complicit in what had happened.

Not that she would.

Too much integrity in her bones.

It would be completely against her grain not to deliver the full measure of whatever she took on—work, marriage, coming out of a cake. That kind of absolute commitment made the thought of having sex with her even more exciting. He'd had a taste of what it would be like. He wanted more. Much more.

Spurred into pursuing this aim, Jake went looking for Harold, finding him in the kitchen, overseeing preparations for dinner. He requested a private word and explained the need to expedite Ms Rossi's departure from her ex-fiancé's home tonight.

'Are you sure this is Ms Rossi's wish?' Harold queried, frowning over Jake's plan.

'I advised it and promised I'd execute it,' Jake stated unequivocally, giving the butler a wise man to man look. 'It is a matter of sensitivity, as you must understand, Harold. Ms Rossi is in the library, breaking off her engagement to my grandfather. Once it's done…'

'Yes, I do see where you're coming from, Mr Jake, but—' he shook his head '—I'm not sure this hasty decision would meet with Mr Byron's approval.'

'A clean cut is always best, Harold,' Jake asserted.

'I suppose the packing up can always be undone, should it not be desired after all,' the older man mused. 'And it would expedite matters if events turn that way…'

How else could they turn, Jake thought impatiently. Obviously the butler just didn't like taking these orders from him, even though he must know they were appropriate in the circumstances.

'Very well,' Harold finally decided. 'If you'll unlock your car, Mr Jake, I'll have Ms Rossi's belongings carried out to it. I will be very sorry to see her go. Such a lovely, lively young woman…'

'Who didn't mean to make a mistake but did,' Jake cut in, wanting action, not more words.

It raised the older man's eyebrows. 'I imagine it would be very easy for a young lady to make a mistake with you, Mr Jake.'

'The mistake was with my grandfather, not me,' Jake retorted in some exasperation.

The butler had the last word. 'Well, sir, that is a matter of opinion. If you'll excuse me, I'll go and supervise the packing.'

The clinch in the main reception had not been a mistake! Jake churned over Harold's point of view as he went outside to unlock the Ferrari. He was very fond of his grandfather. He hoped the old man would not be too offended by his actions tonight. All was fair in love and war, and he'd given fair warning that he considered Melissa Rossi *his* woman right at the initial meeting between her and his grandfather at the birthday party.

If Merlina had not been in such a perverse mood, throwing her independence in his face, and his grandfather backing her up because it suited him, this whole affair would not have got off the ground. He was simply getting her back where she belonged. With him. No mistake about that!

Although he had to concede his grandfather might very well be besotted, given that he had proposed marriage. On the other hand, how could any of his marriages be taken seriously when none of them had lasted beyond a few years?

The discomfiting idea that Merlina might have made the spring/autumn relationship work flitted through his mind. She was a very strong-minded woman. And his grandfather was eighty years old. Maybe he'd seen this as his sunset marriage and would be very aggrieved with Jake for breaking it up.

'Damn, damn, damn!' he muttered, realising his action tonight might well have landed him in a very thorny place. Best he face up to it, too. No whizzing Merlina away without speaking to his grandfather first—find out how troubled the waters were and do his best not to pour oil onto them.

He took a few deep calming breaths of the cooler night air as he waited by the Ferrari to load whatever had to be loaded in the trunk. It couldn't be much, unless the shopping spree at Double Bay had been over-the-top extravagant. He'd cram it in anyway, leaving Merlina no excuse to come back.

Impatience pumped through him, making it seem like forever before his grandfather's valet—the invaluable Vincent—appeared, carrying an overnight case and a bunch of boutique bags. 'Is that all of it?' Jake asked, moving quickly to open the trunk.

'Of course, sir. I never miss anything,' Vincent answered loftily.

'Well, you'll be missing Ms Rossi very shortly,' Jake slung at him, out of temper with the situation.

'That will be a great pity,' Vincent remarked, stowing the bags, then stepping back to give a reproving look. 'Mr Byron has been very happy since Ms Rossi has come to stay.'

'It's not even been *three* days!' Jake snapped, inwardly

rebelling against the guilt building up in him. He was not used to feeling guilty about anything.

'At Mr Byron's age, *every* happy day is precious. Perhaps you are too young to appreciate that, sir.'

Having delivered this insidious hit, Vincent turned on his heel and marched back into the mansion.

Jake slammed the trunk shut, locked the Ferrari again and strode after him. Merlina had certainly had time enough to break the news to his grandfather. Why she was still lingering in the library raised a flurry of a gut-churning questions. He had to get in there and set everything straight, make sure she came away with him tonight.

A sense of urgency drove him into entering the library without knocking. His grandfather was propped against the front of his mahogany desk, looking relaxed and in control of the situation. Merlina was sitting back in the large leather reading chair, looking equally at ease with her legs crossed and her arms draped loosely on the arm-rests. It instantly struck Jake there was no tension in the air, not a smidgeon of distress. It was as though they were simply enjoying a chat together.

'What's going on?' he demanded.

The curt tone raised his grandfather's eyebrows. 'I might ask the same question of you, Jake? You come here on the pretence of needing help at work...'

'I did miss Merlina at work.'

The vehement claim provoked an ironic little smile. 'No doubt you did. Nevertheless, does that excuse applying all your dynamic sex appeal to take her away from me?'

Jake felt a wave of guilty heat scorch up his neck. 'I'm sorry but she shouldn't marry you, Pop.' He glared at Merlina. 'Haven't you told him that?'

'Yes, I did,' she answered wryly, waving her left hand for him to see the huge flashy diamond. 'I offered to give Byron back his ring…'

She was still wearing it!

'I've persuaded Merlina to hold on to it,' his grandfather went on.

'Why?' Jake thundered, a mountain of confusion and frustration welling up and crushing all sense of guilt.

'My boy, I've lived long enough to be worldly about these little peccadillos. Just a flash in the pan, so to speak. It will burn out in what? Three months at most? What's your judgement on this, Merlina?'

She sighed. 'Maybe three months, Byron.'

'And what if it isn't?' Jake grated.

'I can wait,' his grandfather said blithely. 'When it's over and she's feeling sad and sorry, I'll be happy to cheer her up again.'

'Don't count on it being over in a hurry,' Jake warned, the violence he'd felt earlier raging through him again, spurring him on to say, 'I might just marry Merlina myself.'

It shocked his grandfather out of his confidence. 'You don't mean that.'

Merlina also gaped at him in surprise. 'And give up your playboy life?'

'We'll talk about that if we come to it,' Jake threw at her, instinctively shying away from such a total commitment. He addressed his grandfather, wanting this irksome confrontation ended. 'I'm sorry for putting you out but you shouldn't have rushed into this breach, Pop. Merlina and I had a connection going before you met her and I'm not about to walk away from it.'

'Seems to me you didn't appreciate her enough. Don't forget that I will, Merlina,' came the swift counter-argument.

'Just butt out of this, Pop!' Jake demanded in exasperation. 'Merlina, I've got your things in my car. Let's go now. Enough has been said.'

No argument, which was some relief. She rose obligingly from her chair, but then he had to suffer through her going to his grandfather, kissing him on the cheek and saying warmly, 'Thanks for everything, Byron. You've been very kind.'

'You will always be a pleasure to me, my dear,' came the benevolent reply. 'Take care. My grandson still has a lot of growing up to do.'

Jake's jaw clenched. He wasn't about to stay and argue that point here and now. His primary goal was get Merlina away and obliterate any chance of her reconsidering a marriage to his grandfather, who was still clearly capable of charming birds off trees.

At last he had her arm securely tucked around his for the walk out to his car. She was coming with him willingly enough, but the ostentatious ring on her engagement finger was still glinting provocatively at him. Not for long, he vowed. Before they went to bed together, he would make her take it off.

Then he would make damned sure she would never want to put it on again!

CHAPTER EIGHT

I MIGHT just marry her myself...

He'd said it. He'd actually said it. The big M word. Merlina tried reasoning that the stunning declaration had emerged under extreme provocation, but her mind was dizzy with the possibility that Jake could mean it. He surely wouldn't say it just to get her back working for him, and it didn't seem likely that he'd say it to win against his grandfather. It was too *big*.

With her head whirling and her insides wildly tremulous at being physically connected to Jake again as he walked her out to his car, Merlina couldn't help feeling thrilled at the forceful purpose in his every step, his determination to carry her along with him. He wanted to be attached to her. He wanted to be intimate with her. And only three days ago she had given up on Jake and his free-wheeling world.

Had she been right to play Byron's game?

In a way, it had been like tricking Jake into rushing down a path he might not have normally taken, and she was still carrying on a deception with Byron's engagement ring. Yet if she hadn't done it, would she have ever had a chance of getting this close to Jake Devila? A chance of marrying him? On the other hand, would he make a good husband? Would he be a good father? How could she believe it?

Right now he was helping her into the passenger seat of his red Ferrari. The flashy sports car did not suggest the psyche of a family man. Completely the opposite, in fact. It was probably crazy to think about marrying him. An affair was definitely on the cards and Merlina couldn't deny she was terribly tempted by the exciting experience of having Jake as a lover. But she was nervous about it, too. He'd had so many women. How would she compare?

He shut the car door and swiftly strode around the bonnet to take the driver's seat. The tall, athletic *maleness* of him shot quivers through her stomach. She would soon have the chance to see him naked, feel him naked. So many times she had fantasised such a scene taking place. Now that the hot, hard reality of it was rushing in on her, she was scared of it.

Jake settled beside her and closed his door, filling the space inside the car with a sense of primal urgency. He gunned the powerful engine and they were away, charging into a togetherness they had never had before. The security gates at the end of the driveway were being opened but he had to slow the car briefly and he reached across and took her hand, his fingers tightening around hers in a possessive grasp.

'Are you okay, Merlina?' he asked in a surprisingly gentle tone.

His dark eyes scanned hers for some sign that she was with him in spirit as well as physically present.

'I don't know,' she answered shakily. 'Taking off with you feels like a rash leap in the dark.'

He squeezed her hand reassuringly. 'Don't worry. Just let it happen.'

'Don't you ever think about what you're doing, Jake?'

'I don't have to think about this. It's right between us. You know it is.'

His eyes blazed absolute conviction at her, then satisfied that he'd settled that point, he removed his hand to shift gears and turned his gaze to the street they were about to enter.

'It wasn't right until I turned into a blonde for the cake act,' she muttered. Which reminded her… 'What happened with Vanessa Hall? You were in the middle of a relationship with her.'

'Vanessa and I called it quits on Saturday.'

'Because of me?'

'Yes. Because of you.' He threw her a quick burning glance. 'Let it be understood that Vanessa was no more than a social convenience in my life.'

'And I was a work convenience,' spilled out in a bitter little burst.

'No. You were *never* a convenience,' he denied emphatically.

'What was I then?' she challenged, still needing to probe his feelings for her.

'The light of my life. How's that?' He flashed her a grin, getting back into his playboy stride. 'And I'm not about to let it go out.'

Was it a bit of flippant charm or did he mean it? 'When did I become the light of your life?' she asked, mockingly adding, 'Suddenly? On Saturday afternoon?'

The grin turned into a grimace of vexation at her reading of the situation. 'This is no flash in the pan, Merlina. In fact, the chemistry we mixed together stirred to life at your job interview with me, strengthened considerably on your first day at work and has been running on well-charged batteries ever since. And for you to pull the plug on it…' His dark eyebrows beetled down at her. 'Why did you?'

She shrugged, feeling more able to cope with this conversation. Silence fed too many doubts and worries. 'I was sick of being your wind-up doll,' she answered bluntly.

'Hmm…I always anticipated your calling it time up sooner or later. '

That stung her into saying, 'Oh, really? I thought you expected me to sparkle for you as long as you liked.'

'No, I was just seeing how far I could wind you. I thought you might explode over the cake idea. I was actually looking forward to the conflagration, but you held it in and paid me out on your own spectacular terms—a tactic, I might add, that I admired for its sheer boldness until my grandfather leapt on board and cut me out.'

'You weren't *in*, Jake. You were with Vanessa Hall,' she reminded him cattily, remembering how many times she'd burned over his women. It was all very well to call her the light of his life. What were they? Briefly flickering candles?

'Believe me. Vanessa was well aware of how *in* I was by the end of Saturday's party,' he drawled sardonically.

'What? You had to lose me before you decided you wanted me?' Merlina sniped, disgruntled with his two-faced attitude.

'I told you. It was always there. But you were so good at working with me I didn't want to complicate the situation.'

'Right! So it was okay to keep me dangling to serve your interests. Never mind how I felt about it.'

His attention instantly veered from the road to focus intently on her. 'How did you feel about it?'

Merlina clamped her mouth shut. Those treacherous words had slipped out. She knew better than to give anything up to Jake Devila. He'd go to work on it and get an advantage for himself. She had to keep her obsession with him hidden and try to find the real guts in what he was now revealing.

'I don't like being played with,' she tossed at him. 'I don't know what I'm doing here with you. I should have stayed with Byron.'

'No!'

'You're just going to play with me on another level, Jake.'

'It ceased to be a game the moment you threw down the gauntlet, Merlina,' he said with surprising seriousness.

'What is it then? Isn't this all about winning what you want?'

'No. It's about sharing something special.' His eyes pinned hers in a brief glittering challenge. 'Something that neither of us will get from anyone else.'

She sucked in a quick breath to ease the tight squeeze on her heart. It was what scared her most, never being able to find anyone else who could touch the chords in her that Jake touched—touched and tweaked and tuned to his pitch. Instinct told her he would have even more power over her feelings if she went to bed with him. Yet if she didn't…maybe she would be missing the most special experience of her entire life.

'I'm not sure I believe it would be anything special to you, Jake,' she said on a doubtful sigh. 'Perhaps you think you can seduce me back to work with you.'

He said nothing.

Which, to Merlina's mind, meant she'd hit the nail on the head. Except he threw her into emotional confusion again when he did reply.

'Seduction is not my scene. I've only ever been with women who've wanted to be with me. I hope you will choose to be my partner at work again because we make a great team. And I don't think anyone can fill your shoes, Merlina.'

Those all too seductive words completely destroyed the cynicism she had struggled to maintain. She wanted to be his partner—his partner in everything. They did make a great team. And she knew in her bones that no one was going to fill his shoes, either.

The need to be with him dragged at her heart. She closed her eyes, wishing it was possible to forget everything else and just let it happen. She could give it three months, couldn't she? If it didn't look like leading where she wanted it to go, break it off then and walk away. But having got in so deep, would she want to?

The choices one made directed one's life, but how many choices were driven by emotion? Had she really chosen to carve out a career for herself, or was it simply a rebellion against the constrictions innate in living up to *the Italian way*, as dictated by her father. Had she chosen to cut her hair and re-image herself to get the job at Signature Sounds or had that motivation been pushed by the desire to make Jake Devila sit up and take notice of her—man/woman notice?

As for playing the get-Jake game with Byron, she'd been indulging a vengeful streak that had completely overwhelmed common sense. Vengeance and hope—a cocktail for chaos, not a recipe for forging a good future.

Her resignation from the job had been an attempt to take real control of where she was going in her life, yet even that had been a reaction to intolerable circumstances, and this move from Jake tonight was spinning her right out of control again. Her head was aching from the stress of trying to choose the *right* direction. Her heart kept thumping its own message—*let it happen. You want it to.*

Jake was acutely conscious of her silence. Had he said enough to break the barriers she was trying to keep between them? She wasn't arguing and Mel—Merlina—was rarely lost for words when she had a point to push. He had to stop thinking Mel. If he slipped up on her name again, she'd probably kick him out of her life.

A quick glance told him she'd closed her eyes, retreating into her own inner world, shutting him out. That was a bad sign. Her mind was probably working against him, thinking of Vanessa and the other women who'd traipsed through his life and bed since she'd been his personal assistant. He couldn't blame her for not believing she held a uniquely special place in his mind. But she did. He'd just wanted to keep her separate from the party scene—all to himself at work.

No choice now.

He had to do whatever had to be done not to lose her.

They were crossing the harbour bridge. Only fifteen more minutes to her apartment in Chatswood. He knew where it was, had dropped her there a few times after meetings with business associates had run late. She'd never invited him in and he'd never pushed to go in, knowing it would be a dangerous place to be. Too intimate. Too tempting.

But that didn't matter any more. His whole body was yearning to have her in his arms again, firing up the passion that had flared between them. Just kissing her had been pure dynamite. And she had certainly felt it as strongly as he had. She couldn't turn her back on it. No one in their right mind would.

A red traffic light forced a stop at the Artarmon turn-off. It gave him time to take more than a glance at her. She was a study in stillness, as though she was holding herself tightly together. Her eyes were still closed. There was a sad, defeated air about her expressionless face. It suggested she had given up on fighting him but wasn't happy about it.

He wanted to lean over and kiss her, bring her back to vibrant life again. The car behind his honked an impatient warning that the line of traffic in front of him was moving. Jake switched his attention to the road ahead and drove on, telling himself he'd make everything right for Merlina when the trip to Chatswood was over.

The car came to a halt and the engine was switched off. Time up, Merlina thought. No escape from facing up to the situation now. With a resigned sigh, she opened her eyes and saw they were parked directly in front of her apartment. Jake had brought her home as promised.

It was an old-fashioned block of only four apartments and she lived on left-hand side ground floor. She had her own entrance via a front porch which caught the sun in winter. Apart from this pleasant feature, the apartment was fairly basic: a living room which was separated from the kitchen by a breakfast bar, a bathroom/laundry and two bedrooms at the back.

Jake had never been inside. Nor had she ever been inside his penthouse at Milson's Point where he had undoubtedly entertained many women. A convulsive little shiver of revulsion accompanied that thought. Merlina silently vowed she would never go there. If she was going to have sex with him it would take place in her bed where no other intimacy had ever occurred.

Her heart fluttered wildly as Jake alighted from the car and headed for the passenger side. Any second now she would be stepping out beside him and what would happen after that? He opened the door. Merlina was momentarily paralysed with fear, unable to make herself move.

'We're here,' he said, prompting action.

'Right!' she forced herself to say, and somehow managed to swing her legs out of the car.

Jake grasped her arm, assisting in getting her upright from the low-slung seat. It brought her very close to him and when he took hold of her other arm, turning her to face him, every nerve in her body zinged as though hit by an electric charge. Was he about to kiss her? She looked up in helpless agitation. For several fraught moments, his eyes searched hers, and the tension emanating him held her more captive than his hands. What was he looking for? What did he want to find?

He didn't kiss her.

'Go and open up,' he said gruffly. 'I'll get your bags out of the trunk and bring them inside.'

Her arms were released. He turned away. Free to move, Merlina recollected herself and headed for her front door. *I'm his puppet again,* she thought, *acting to his dictation.* She didn't even realise she had no handbag with her until she reached the porch. It was probably in the trunk, too. Rather than turn back, she took the emergency key from the little magnetic box attached to the pot stand under the pink geranium, used it to unlock the door, then returned it to its hiding place.

The trunk slammed shut, which meant Jake was on his way. She entered her living room, leaving the door opened wide for him to carry in the bags of clothes, including the red rose St Valentine's Day bikini, which she'd designed with malice aforethought. Going out with a big bang had probably not been a good idea. Another decision driven by emotion.

Everything was tidy, as she'd left it on Saturday morning. There weren't any red roses in a vase. Jake hadn't sent her any on St Valentine's day. No token of love from him. Only...*unfinished business!*

'Where do you want these?' he asked as he came in.

She couldn't bring herself to direct him to her bedroom. 'Just drop them on the floor, thanks, Jake.'

He pushed the door shut before unloading himself. Merlina didn't have to be Einstein to know he didn't intend to leave in a hurry. Having set down her bags as directed, he straightened up, his presence more dominating than ever now that he was within the four walls of her home.

The tension swirling between them choked her into silence. All she could do was stare at him—this man whom she had craved for so long. Not for just a sexual experience. She desperately wanted him to make love to her—real love—and for it to be so wonderful he'd never want any other woman. A team for life, not limited to work. He'd used the M word...

'Why are you frightened of me?' he asked, frowning in concern, his hands lifting, palms open in an appeal for belief that he meant her no harm.

'Because...' It was a croak. She swallowed hard. 'Because...' Again she stopped, her head whirling with reasons, but voicing them would sound like begging for more than he was ever likely to give and that would leave her totally defenceless.

'You didn't really answer me before,' he said, his eyes demanding the truth now, though his voice held a caring gentleness as he repeated the question. 'Are you a virgin, Merlina?'

'No. But…it's been a while…' *Like years.* Her mind suddenly seized on a reason that any woman with any sense should be thinking of in this situation. 'And I'm not protected.'

The words were no sooner out than she realised they implied she was not against having sex with him, only that she wasn't *prepared* for it tonight.

He smiled in relief as he assured her, 'I'll take care of it.'

Of course, she thought caustically. He was probably in the habit of carrying a pocketful of condoms. Who knew when lust would jump up and bite you, and it would be highly inconvenient if he got a woman pregnant. She was crazy to be dallying with a playboy.

'Don't worry about anything,' he soothed as he moved forward, his natural confidence restored, flashing his dimples in distracting fashion while she stood like a dummy, letting him come to her.

He slid one arm around her waist and lifted his other hand to her face, his fingers grazing softly down her cheek, tracing her lips with tantalising tenderness. Again all Merlina could do was stare at him. His eyes were promising her pleasure she had never known before, and there was no longer any question of whether or not to surrender to temptation.

The promise was too close, beaming into her tormented soul, tugging her irresistibly into abandoning her fears and following his lead…*the light of her life.*

CHAPTER NINE

THE swell of caring Jake felt was completely new to him. None of the women he had ever been with had shown any inhibitions about having sex with him. The poignant vulnerability in Merlina's eyes was so suggestive of innocence, he was certain her sexual experience had been very limited, and probably not pleasurable enough to seek repetition. She wasn't even on the Pill. That alone spoke volumes.

It made him acutely conscious that this was not a casual tumble into bed. Not for her. Not for him, either. It was make or break time. If he didn't get it right for her, didn't make her feel good about giving herself to him, she might wipe him off as a big mistake. Might even go back to his grandfather.

Her lips quivered under his feather-light finger touch, parting slightly as she sucked in a deep breath. There were no sparks of fiery amber in her eyes. The brown had darkened into pools of dark chocolate—huge eyes swimming with unbridled emotion that tugged at his heart, asking silent questions which he knew he had to answer. Somehow.

Her hands had lifted to his chest, not to push him away, but resting there tentatively, not quite prepared to actively encourage more physical intimacy, yet he could feel the taut waiting in her body, the wanting for him to take the initiative, *to make it happen.*

The moment he kissed her he knew they would slide up around his neck, holding him tight as she had in his grandfather's home. But there was no longer any need to prove the existence of the sexual chemistry between them and he didn't want to move fast this time.

He wanted to explore every facet of Merlina Rossi, know all that she was, far beyond what she'd shown him at work. Her smooth olive skin had made him wonder how it would feel. His finger pads revelled in its satin softness as he slid them across her cheek and into her hair, so thick and glossy, like massed strands of silk, not the often dry texture of dyed blond hair.

What was it about blondes that had attracted him? Maybe it was a come-hither attitude embodied in their wish to be more attractive to men. Whereas Merlina... *This is me,* she had cried when he had accused her of adopting a different image to the one he had insisted upon for her job as his P.A. If he had not demanded the change, if her hair had remained long, how gloriously sensual it would be to lie on it, to have it brushing over his body!

'I shouldn't have told you to have it cut,' he said regretfully.

Her head leaned into the cup of his hand, rubbing it like a cat that loved being stroked. 'It doesn't matter,' she said huskily. 'I can grow it again now.'

Be herself...away from him.

The intolerable thought spurred the need to draw her into a closeness she wouldn't want to break. His mouth sought the response from hers she had given before, using all its erotic skill to excite her out of the passive stance she'd been holding. Her arms instantly flew up to wind around his neck. Her tongue danced a wild tango with his. The voluptuous swell of her breasts pressed against his chest, their hard peaks imprinting proof of her arousal.

He gathered her closer and her wonderfully soft and curvaceous femininity was an intoxicating pleasure. *Skinny* was great for wearing designer clothes. Feeling pelvic bones and ribs was not so sexy. Merlina's body was sensually perfect and his hands revelled in moulding it to his.

He was on fire for her, desire roaring through him, tightening his muscles, making his erection shriek *now, now, now!* He barely leashed the urge to race her off to bed. Fast was wrong. She'd think he only cared about getting sexual relief, using her to do it. If she'd only had selfish lovers, adding himself to that list wouldn't win him any stay of judgement on her leaving him to his own life. He had to ease back, slow down, stay in control.

Merlina was so caught up in the throes of passion, a guttural little moan of protest scraped from her throat when he withdrew his mouth from hers, bringing a halt to the intense flow of excitement.

'It's all right,' he soothed, whispering the words in her ear, making it tingle as he tucked her head into the curve of his neck and shoulder, then rubbed his cheek softly over her hair. 'You'll have me exploding if I don't take a breather.'

A gurgle of laughter bubbled out, erupting from the relief of having him dismiss the nervous fear that she was an inadequate kisser compared to the more experienced women he'd been with.

'You think it's funny?' he queried in a wry tone.

'No…no…' She scooped in a quick breath and planted

a happy kiss on his throat. 'I think it's great,' she murmured with a rush of heartfelt pleasure at having him find her so desirable.

'Oh, you like having that kind of power over me, do you?' he said teasingly.

A wild recklessness seized her. Suddenly freed from the dreadful bank of inhibitions that had previously almost paralysed her, she lifted her head back and grinned at him. 'Yes, I do.'

He laughed as though he loved the unexpected burst of honesty from her. His eyes sparkled with wicked mischief. 'You're challenging me to drive you into the same state of urgency.'

'You've done a fair job so far,' she said archly, entering into his playboy game. It was who Jake was, and nothing was going to change him, so why not let herself enjoy it for once?

'Fair…' he repeated assessingly, his eyes gathering dangerous glints of sexual intent. 'An escalation is definitely needed here. I think I'll start by getting rid of this belt which has been sticking into me.'

He swiftly dropped his embrace, his hands deftly undoing the plaited rosette which fastened the soft leather tie around her waist. Her stomach contracted as the belt loosened and dropped to the floor. This was the first stage of undressing. *Don't think ahead,* she fiercely told herself. *Just let it happen.*

But as he disconnected the hook and eye which kept the wrap-around silk dress in place, she desperately wished she was wearing a sexy suspender belt and stockings instead of plain, comfortable pantihose. The creamy silk bra and knickers were okay, not exactly alluring but she liked them and if Jake was used to more exotic female underwear, well…tough luck! Surely getting down to basics was the aim, anyway, and she wasn't ashamed of her body.

'Mmm…silk hair, silk dress, silk bra,' he purred approvingly, his hand shifting the dress aside enough to slide under the fabric and close around the fullness of one achingly sensitive breast. His mouth curved into a very sensual smile, his eyes simmering with sexy appreciation. 'What does that tell me about you, Merlina?'

She wanted to close her own eyes and just feel him feeling her, focus inwardly on the gently kneading fingers, the tantalising sweep of his thumb over her extremely erect nipple, the intense pleasure flooding from his touch. Yet if she did so, wouldn't it tell him how deeply he was affecting her? Better to keep the banter going, treat everything lightly.

'That I'm a silk worm and you should feed me mulberry leaves?' she tossed out.

He laughed, delight dancing over his face, dimples flashing, and the hand caressing her breast forgot its seductive intent and squeezed in avid possession as he sobered and said, 'I'd rather feed you me.'

Her heart slammed around her chest at the suggestive imagery of those words. Somehow her mind was still alert enough to zap out a snappy reply. 'Careful, Jake! I might chew you into little bits.'

'Well, you'd only do that if you found me tasty.'

'Or too difficult to swallow.'

'Guess we have to test that out.'

A joyous confidence glowed from him. His hands started sliding around her back and Merlina knew her bra was about to be slipped from its moorings. Attacked by another panicky wave of vulnerability, she wildly seized on a bold move of her own.

'You're wearing too many clothes for tasting,' she pointed out, hoping to put him on the *naked* spot first.

He grinned. 'Did I ever tell you I love the way your mind works?'

Love? That one word rattled all the skeletons in Merlina's emotional closet. She barely caught breath enough to say, 'No, you never did.'

'Always put me on my mettle. Thrust, parry, thrust...exciting stuff.'

Not exciting enough to want to be with me all the time, she thought rebelliously, telling herself not to get sucked into the *love* pit. That was too dangerous with Jake. Besides, her defensive tactic had worked. Instead of undoing her bra, his hands had whipped down to the bottom of his shirt, which he was gathering up for lift-off. She quickly removed her arm-lock on his head and stood looking on in awed fascination as he not only stripped off his shirt but all his other clothes, as well.

Her stomach felt weirdly hollow as her eyes skated down his magnificent, male physique and fastened on the sexual equipment which was certainly primed for action. With her this time. Forget the women he'd had in the past, she fiercely told herself. *She* had put him in this high state of arousal and despite common sense cautioning her to keep everything light, a primitive sense of possessiveness was clawing through her, wanting to take and hold and forge an inseparable connection with Jake Devila.

Her man.

For tonight, anyway.

Though maybe it would stretch into months.

And what then?

Stop thinking about that.

*Just take what you can...what's on offer right now...
reach out and take it...*

'Merlina...?'

He was asking her to. She could hear it in his voice, asking why she wasn't touching, wasn't tasting. But she couldn't make herself do it. Her hands were clenching and unclenching at her sides instead of moving forward. It wasn't a game. Not for her, it wasn't. She couldn't play it as though it was.

'Don't be frightened of me.'

His voice was soft, serious, tapping at the truth. Before she could find wits enough to answer, to brush the idea of fear aside, he moved, sliding her dress from her shoulders. It slithered down her arms and dropped to the floor, pooling around her feet. Then his arms were around her again, drawing her into a terribly intimate embrace and she knew she'd gone past the point of no return, and everything within her quivered an acceptance of it.

He rested his forehead against hers and gruffly murmured, 'It will be all right. I promise you.'

Then her bra was gone and her bare breasts were making contact with his naked chest—a smooth hairless chest that heaved with a swift intake of air, making her acutely aware of its muscled strength and the enticing heat of his taut flesh. He tilted her head back and kissed her slowly, sensuously, not so much seeking to excite but transmitting an assurance that he could and would go gently with her.

The caring implicit in the kiss sent a rush of soothing warmth to her torn heart. She wrapped her arms around his neck, pressing closer, revelling in the wildly erotic freedom of feeling of her skin against his, the exhilarating vibrancy that shot through her whole body in anticipation of feeling more and more.

His hands glided down the curve of her back and under her pantihose and knickers, his thumbs hooking over their waist-bands, smoothly drawing the flimsy garments past her hips, lower, lower, his fingers curling under her bottom, lifting her into a more flagrant, sexually charged fit with him.

Chaotic excitement broke loose. Her mouth sucked his tongue in hard, instinctively pursuing the blind need to have him deep inside her. He instantly reciprocated, propelling a driving urgency that he suddenly cut off, retreating to tantalising nibbles on her lips.

'Not yet, not yet,' he breathed raggedly. 'Let's get these off.'

He bent quickly, peeling the last of her clothes down her quivering thighs. His head dropped through the loop of her arms, leaving her hands grabbing onto his shoulders, needing the support as he lifted her feet, one after another, removing her shoes, stripping her completely naked like him. Her body shivered at the sudden loss of his heat. She was light-headed, dizzy.

It was sheer blissful relief when he simply picked her up, cradling her tightly against his chest as he straightened to his full height again, one arm hooked around her thighs, the other supporting her back. Her head nestled happily on his shoulder while he trailed soft kisses over her hair, his mouth moving down to her ear, blowing an erotic waft of warm air into it, making her heart leap and race with excitement.

'Your bedroom, Merlina…where is it?' he murmured.

'Last door at the end of the hall,' she answered without the slightest hesitation, wanting him to take her there, wanting *everything* to happen with this man.

Her hands glided over his strongly muscled back as he carried her down the hall. He was so gorgeously male—all of him—and somehow that made her feel more intensely female, stirring the primal instincts no amount of civilisation could retrain. They had broken loose and were zinging through her, exulting in the promise of what was to come.

He opened the door to her bedroom, switched on the light. *Yes*, she thought wildly, *let there be light.* She wanted the visual pleasure of seeing him, watching him—Jake Devila, pumped up with desire for her and acting on it, intent on sweeping her along with him.

He laid her on the scarlet silk doona she had brought back from China—a tourist trip she had taken after leaving her last job. Buying the doona had been total self-indulgence but she'd loved it on sight, the brilliant scarlet printed so exotically with graceful sprays of flowers and pagodas and Chinese ladies in traditional dress, carrying pretty shade umbrellas and walking over curved bridges which invariably featured in the Chinese gardens the tour group had visited. She'd bought the matching pillow slips, as well, unable to resist the complete set.

Having it—using it—had been a private pleasure, yet now as Jake stood back, his gaze travelling slowly over the vision she made with the scarlet silk spread underneath her, she was glad to have surprised him with something extraordinary, elated that he looked at her as though she was the perfect centrepiece for such sensuous splendour. But she didn't want him standing apart from her.

Acting instinctively to draw him to her, she slithered her body over the silk, stretching out invitingly, seductively, taking a feline satisfaction in feeling it against her skin, though it was Jake's skin she wanted to feel most, moving against hers. Her eyes passionately burned their own message at him—*Come to me…me…*

* * *

Jake was momentarily stunned. The sight of a woman on a bed had never before checked the need which was still rampaging through him, but Merlina...the glorious beauty of her had made him pause. The soft, voluptuous curves were all woman. As a woman was meant to be, he thought, the images of art masterpieces running through his mind, wonderful nudes posed in opulent settings. Her lovely smooth skin gleamed like satin. Satin against silk. Red silk. So incredibly sexy. Like a fantasy. Though the marvellous female mystique would have been heightened if only...

'Mad...stupid...' he muttered, shaking his head over the blind error in judgement he'd made. 'Why didn't I see?'

The compulsive yearning in Merlina's heart skipped into panicky bewilderment. 'See what?' spilled straight off her tongue, the need to know how he was thinking jerking through her mind.

'I was so wrong. Long hair was right for you. It should be cascading all over these pillows.' He stretched out on the bed beside her, propping himself up on one elbow as he softly raked the shorter spill of her layered hair back behind her ear. 'Forgive me for being an arrogant fool.'

A tidal wave of relief.

Plus the unexpected burst of humility from Jake shook the playboy wall she had built around him. It made him more human, more accessible as a person. 'You didn't know me, Jake,' she said, hoping, fiercely willing him to take that step, making her different—*uniquely* different—to all the other women he'd taken to bed. She so desperately wanted to be the special one…the one he'd love…the one he'd marry…

His eyes searched hers with deeply probing intensity, feeding the hope, making it swell until it bubbled through her mind like champagne. 'Who is this woman I see now?' he murmured, his voice gruff with emotions he wasn't expressing but they certainly suggested more than a passing lust for her. 'What else have you kept hidden from me, Merlina?'

Happiness gushed through her like a fountain bursting into brilliant play. She lifted one arm up around his neck and ran her hand into *his* hair, revelling in touching him, feeling him, wanting to wind her fingers through the thick waves and into his mind, touch him there, as well, touch him deeply.

'Nothing that wasn't there for you to find if you'd been truly interested in looking,' she said softly, her eyes—the windows to her soul—wide-open to him. 'You put the image you wanted between us, Jake.'

'I don't want that image back,' he declared emphatically. 'I want the real you.'

Did he see the joy erupting in her soul—the joy she couldn't contain? 'I'm here,' she said simply, offering herself up to be loved.

A smile of sheer devilment broke across his face and his eyes were suddenly steaming with plans he intended to execute with maximum impact in mind. 'Yes,' he said with relish. 'Here with me. Let's make that in every sense there is.'

Did he really mean every sense or was he only talking in the sexual sense? For a moment Merlina felt a little flicker of disappointment. She'd opened a door to him and it seemed he was side-stepping, but she had no time to think about it. He kissed her, instantly drawing her back into a world of vibrant sensation, bombarding her with such intense excitement it was impossible not to give herself up to it.

He kissed the pulse at the base of her throat, heating her entire bloodstream. He kissed her breasts, his tongue swirling around her nipples, lashing them into peaks of hard need, then sucking them into his mouth, making a wildly erotic feast of taste and titillation that drove her into offering them up for more of it, her own hands sliding under and lifting the soft flesh, wantonly aiding and abetting the exquisite ravishment, totally enthralled by it.

But he didn't stay there. He moved lower, sweeping kisses over her stomach, teasing her navel with his tongue, grazing his mouth over the erogenous zones under her hip-bones, causing her skin to twitch with pleasure, his hands caressing her legs apart, long, shiver-inducing, purposeful caresses on her inner thighs, and the tension of becoming more and more intimately exposed to him had every nerve and muscle in her body poised on a very fine edge in anticipation of being touched *there*, and taken to even more extremes of feeling.

Her stomach was contracting. Her heart was drumming in her ears. Her breathing was reduced to quick panting, her mind seized with the waiting, the knowing it would come, focussed totally on how it would be, her eyes shut tight, instinctively closing out everything else so that her entire being was tuned to this inner world of Jake's making.

She felt his fingers slide slowly between the folds of her sex, seeking the source of the moist heat that surely told him how wildly aroused she was. They circled the highly sensitive opening while his thumb laid bare her clitoris, caressing it into a stiff pulsing peak, which he then covered with his mouth, licking, sucking, making her body arch with almost torturous tension.

She couldn't bear it. Couldn't…

Her hands scrambled into his hair, tugging, begging an end to it. Her inner muscles were convulsing, her nerves screaming, yet she cried out at the loss of the strangely sweet torment as he released her from it, lifting himself up to position himself for the plunge into ultimate intimacy.

Her hands kneaded his back muscles in desperate wanting. Her legs curled around his taut buttocks, her feet urging him to a fast entry. The need was so compelling, nothing else existed for her. She hated the enforced pause for him to slide on a condom, savagely wished there'd been no need for it. But it was sheer bliss when he came into her, filling the aching void. The relief of it sent ripples of pleasure through her entire body. She felt herself pulsing around him, melting, and the glorious heavenliness of it put an ecstatic smile on her face.

'Don't hide from me, Merlina. Open your eyes.'

He was deep inside her, beautifully wonderfully deep. It was difficult to tear her concentration away from how it felt, yet Jake was giving her this pleasure. It wasn't fair to keep it to herself. She opened her eyes, not even thinking of what she might see in his.

'You're smiling,' he said, smiling right back at her, happy that she was happy with him.

'Feels good,' she said, only just stopping herself from blurting out that she *loved* the sense of having him like this.

'Only good?' he quizzed, his smile tilting into a teasing quirk.

'Great?' she offered, wishing he wasn't asking for a rating of his performance. It smacked of playboy games and this was no game to her. She wanted to think this was more than just sex for him—an important connection that was being heightened, deepened by the physical union.

'Great is good but—' the joyous twinkles in his eyes fused into a look of burning purpose '—I aim to improve on that.'

His mouth claimed hers in a kiss of driving passion, his tongue invading strongly, then matching the plunging rhythm of his body, reinforcing his possession, doubling the intense intimacy. Merlina was swamped with wave after wave of incredible sensation, taking her to the crest of climax and spilling her into it, over and over again.

Her arms and legs were suffused with a weird weakness. She couldn't hold on. Jake slid an arm under her to keep her with him, keep the momentum going. It was awesome, fantastic, the constant chaotic roll to pinnacles of creamy pleasure. If this was *just sex* she didn't care. She'd take this blissful ride with Jake wherever it went.

She couldn't imagine anything more exciting, but there was. His body tension seemed to explode into a much faster pumping, and she knew his control had been stretched to the limit. Somehow the sense that he was losing it—*in her*—was wildly exhilarating, and when she felt the spasms of his release, a huge swell of satisfaction triggered a very primal possessiveness. Jake…hers…and her own inner muscles suddenly leapt into squeezing tightly, holding *him* there.

He carried her with him as he rolled onto his side, still maintaining their union with a gentle rocking, one of her legs lying between his, the other loosely hooked over his thigh. Breath whooshed out of his lungs and he scooped in more before moving his mouth over hers in sensual little kisses.

'Tell me it was right for you,' he murmured against her lips.

Right? The question rolled around her dazed mind. It didn't matter any more whether it was right or not. 'Yes,' she said on a contented sigh. It was the truth, no problem at all for her to say it and if Jake wanted to hear it…right at this moment she wanted whatever Jake wanted.

He moved his head back onto the pillow and smiled at her, his dimples deepening, warm pleasure dancing in his eyes. 'You see? You had to be with me, Merlina.'

'Yes,' she said, not even caring if this was only about *winning* for Jake.

'Stay right here!' He dropped a kiss on her forehead as he slowly disentangled himself. 'Got to go to the bathroom. Where is it?'

'First door along the hall.'

'Be back in a minute.'

Getting rid of the condom. He'd kept his promise about protection. Even so, she would feel safer taking a contraceptive pill if they were to have an ongoing relationship.

The back view of Jake as he strode away was just as awesome as the rest of him—a perfectly proportioned male physique. Surely every woman he'd ever been with had wanted to hold on to him. She was no different. She could only hope she was different in Jake's mind—a woman *he* wanted to hold on to.

He moved into the hall, out of sight. She heard the bathroom door being opened. A few moments later the sound of another door being opened made her wonder why he was checking out the guest bedroom.

'Merlina?'

She jack-knifed up from the pillows, shock pumping through her heart.

That was not Jake's voice calling out her name.

It was her father's!

CHAPTER TEN

MERLINA bolted out of bed. She was stark naked. And so was Jake in the bathroom! Their clothes were on the living-room floor. Any second now her father would see them and...a string of loud Italian curses told her he had.

'Merlina, get out here this minute!' came the thunderous command.

'Coming, Papa!' she yelled back, frantically hoping Jake would hear and understand the warning to stay in the bathroom and let her handle her father.

Almost sick with panic, she raced to her clothes cupboard, grabbed her silk dressing-gown off its hanger and put it on as fast as she could. Her hairbrush was in one of the bags Jake had carried in so the best she could do was a finger-comb. It was impossible to make herself look respectable, anyway. Her father was probably still staring at the evidence that she wasn't.

Why, oh, why hadn't he rung the doorbell instead of appropriating the spare key and letting himself in? She would have had time to hide the discarded clothes, time to...but there *was* no time!

On the dubious principle that attack was the best form

of defence, she fronted up to him in the living-room and asked, 'What are you doing here, Papa?'

'What am I doing here?' he repeated incredulously. He threw his hands up in the air in his usual histrionic fashion. His thick, wavy, grey hair was tossed back. The black eyebrows rose, mocking the question. His hawkish nose sniffed the air in battle-readiness. His barrel chest was all puffed out and his teeth—very white against a face darkly weathered by working outside in the vineyard—gnashed before biting out the words again. 'What am I doing here?'

He was starting to sound like a Greek chorus but Merlina knew this was venting in the Italian style, building up to the storm where hail stones would rain on her head.

'You don't usually drop in without warning,' she slid in quickly.

'How can I warn you when you do not answer your telephone?' His dark eyes flashed furious accusation as he wildly gesticulated to punctuate every point he made. 'Not on Saturday. Not on Sunday. Not today. And when we ring your workplace we are told you are not employed there any more. Told by a stranger. No news of this from our daughter.'

'I would have got around to telling you,' she excused, shrugging off the necessity for instant communication about everything—her family's favourite pastime. 'Why were you calling me? Is something wrong at home?'

'And look where this precious independence of yours has got you!' he lashed out with a sweeping gesture of disgust at the clothes on the floor.

Merlina unclenched her jaw, took a deep breath and persisted with her question. 'What's happened? What's brought you here? Is Mamma okay?'

'No, your mother is not okay,' he retorted fiercely. 'She is worried sick about you. All day she is saying, something bad has happened to Merlina. I feel it here.' He slammed his hand over his heart, play-acting her mother's distress. 'I cannot bear it, Angelo, she says. You must fly to Sydney, find her. And what do I find? What do I find?' His arms flew up in outrage again. 'My daughter—' his eyes raked down her red silk dressing-gown '—a scarlet woman!'

Merlina couldn't help rolling her eyes. He'd have her painted as a prostitute next. Banned from his household forever. The modern world and her father had no meeting ground. The big problem was...she didn't want to lose her family. Somehow she had to fight this, but how?

'You've got that wrong, Mr Rossi,' came the calm statement from behind her.

Jake!

She spun around.

He was coming down the hall, a white bath-towel tucked around his waist, but the rest of him still flagrantly naked. Didn't he realise that his appearance would enflame her father's rage? Her heart pitter-pattered in a frenzy of fear over what might happen next.

'So! You've come out of hiding,' her father jeered contemptuously, drawing himself up to match Jake's height and look down his Roman nose at him.

'I wasn't hiding,' Jake corrected him. 'I'd gone to the bathroom and I couldn't help overhearing what was going on out here. Seemed to me I should step in.' He curved his arm around her shoulders in a protective hug. 'I won't have Merlina abused, Mr Rossi.'

Her father glared at him. 'It is you who has abused my daughter, stripping her of her virtue.'

'Papa, please—'

Her plea for some temperance was cut off, her attempt only serving to bring her father's wrath down on her again. 'Who is this man? Did I not teach you to save your virginity for your husband?'

'My name is Jake Devila...'

'Devila?' Enlightenment struck. 'Is that not the name of your employer, Merlina?'

'I don't work for him any more, Papa.'

'What? He sacked you from your job because you let him seduce you into going to bed with him?'

'No, Papa...'

He ignored her denial, attacking Jake again. 'You are a man without honour. Using your position of power over my daughter to turn her mind.'

'He didn't,' Merlina cried. She'd simply given her mind a rest and followed her heart for once.

Her father's finger went up in victorious argument. 'He forced you to have your hair cut. And Sylvana told us he insisted you wear immodest clothes to work.'

'There were good reasons for that,' Merlina almost shouted in her urgent need to be heard. Sylvana's big mouth should have been zippered at birth!

'No. Your father is right,' Jake chimed in. 'I *was* flexing my power.'

Merlina closed her eyes in despair. What was Jake playing at now? He had no idea what her father was like and he was ruining any chance of smoothing over the situation. If, indeed, there was any chance.

'At that point in time, I didn't appreciate that Merlina was perfect the way she was,' he ran on in a quietly diplomatic tone. 'I wanted to fit her into an image that suited

my business. I'm sorry that you found my influence so offensive. It wasn't meant to be.'

'You're sorry?' her father squawked. 'Does that give me
back the daughter you have ruined for any good husband?'

The arm around her shoulders tightened its hug as Jake
picked up her left hand and startled her by holding it out
for her father to see the ring that Byron had put on her third
finger and which was still there, sparkling its solitaire
diamond brilliance. She'd forgotten about it. Byron had
dropped right out of her mind. And for Jake to bring up her
engagement to his grandfather now seemed utter madness.

'I was hoping you would accept me as her husband,
Mr Rossi.'

What?

Merlina's body froze into suspended animation while her
mind spun in wild circles. She feverishly wished Jake had
just spoken the truth. But he might not mean it. He was
trying to get her out of trouble. Trouble that he'd made for
her. Though not entirely. She had been a willing party. But
if he hadn't come after her, brought her home, she'd still be
the *good girl* her father wished her to be, and which she had
been on the whole, within her own sense of right and wrong.

No doubt Jake was thinking they could break the pseu-
do-engagement at a later date. It was Byron's ring, not his,
but her father didn't know that. His eyes were goggling at
the diamond. Hopefully its magnificence was blinding him
to her fall from grace.

'You are engaged to be married?' His wrath had been
considerably appeased by the ring but a frown of disap-
proval was still aimed at Merlina. 'Why did you not tell
him he should ask me for your hand first? Why have you
not brought him to meet the family?'

Her mind boggled over the thought of Jake with her family. They'd eat him alive. He could put on a fine act for her father tonight but her family en masse was another kettle of fish. 'I, er, this has all been very sudden, Papa.'

'Please accept my apology, Mr Rossi,' Jake smoothly appealed. 'With my own parents divorced when I was a child, I didn't appreciate that traditional courtesies would be expected. I surprised Merlina with the ring tonight. We hadn't talked about marriage before. Of course, we know each other very well from having worked closely together for almost two years, but it was only after Merlina resigned, that I've pursued her in a personal sense.'

Oh, wow! He was covering all bases with that little speech. Ironically, all of it was the truth this time, except he was making himself out to be gentleman Jake for her father, not one hint of playboy Jake!

'You did not take advantage of her at work?' her father asked suspiciously.

'I give you my word that nothing untoward happened between us during her employment with me. Completely professional,' came the firm assurance.

Another truth.

Her father gave the situation some hard pondering before finally conceding, 'Then I accept that you are a man of honour.'

'Thank you,' Jake replied respectfully.

'If you are marrying Merlina, you must come and meet the family.'

'Whenever that can be arranged,' Jake replied.

Evasive tactics coming in, Merlina thought. For a moment there he had sounded so sincere, the hope that he might truly mean to marry her had fluttered through her heart. However, the far more credible truth was Jake coming to her rescue, being gallant as a good playboy should when caught out.

'Tomorrow would be very suitable,' her father announced in a challenging tone.

'Tomorrow!' Merlina cried, alarmed at how quickly her father was putting Jake to the test. She desperately wanted to hold onto him, not have him driven away. 'Jake has a business to run, Papa. Tomorrow is a workday.'

'What is more important than family at a time like this?' was hurled back at her. 'Mario's wife has given birth to her baby. Which your mother wished to tell you.'

The telephone calls that she hadn't been here to answer!

But the birth had not been expected for another month. 'That's way too early,' she protested anxiously. 'Is the baby all right? Is Gina all right?'

Her burst of caring seemed to give her father a strong measure of satisfaction. For the first time tonight he spoke to her in a reasonably calm tone. 'Gina is fine. The baby is a little small but he is perfectly healthy.'

'He…a boy this time.' She relaxed into a smile. 'Mario must be pleased.'

'Yes. Three daughters are enough.' Her father glowered pointedly at her. 'Especially when they do not behave as they should.'

'Sorry I was away, Papa…'

'Merlina was with my family, meeting my mother and grandfather,' Jake declared, stepping in to give her absence respectability, having already lifted her up from being a fallen woman.

She heaved a sigh at how adept he was at making their relationship sound official. In fact, he was every bit as good as his grandfather at deception. Unfortunately that was not a happy thought. Deception could achieve a short-term effect, but what would happen when this engagement fell through?

On the family front, she'd probably get sympathy, with Jake cast as a villain for taking her virtue, which she'd supposedly given up in good faith. But what might her brothers do to the absconding husband-to-be? Jake had no idea what he'd just set in motion. Maybe she should spill the real truth, save him from the consequences of his well-meant lies. On the other hand, if there was a possibility…

Hope was a terrible thing.

It held her tongue.

Her father addressed Jake. 'Mario is bringing his wife and baby home tomorrow. We will be holding a family barbecue in the evening. I am inviting you to attend with Merlina.'

Throwing him to the wolves.

Panic drove her to attempt a rescue. 'Papa, I've already explained about work.'

'He's the boss, isn't he? The call is his,' her father insisted aggressively. 'You have met his family. He should meet yours.'

Italian pride!

There was no way to fight it. Jake's *respectable* scenario was reaping what it had sown.

'We'll be there,' he said.

She turned on him in exasperation for jumping straight into the hole she'd been trying to dig him out of. 'It's in Griffith, Jake. That's a six hour drive from Sydney.'

'You can both catch a plane like I did for you, Merlina,' her father persisted.

She swung back to him, frightened of the dilemma he was posing. 'It wasn't for me. It was because Mamma nagged you into it.'

'So? We do these things for our women, do we not?' He tossed this at Jake, testing how deep the devotion was to his daughter.

'Yes, we do,' Jake cheerfully agreed. 'We'll catch a plane to Griffith tomorrow afternoon.'

She could have choked him.

He was escalating something that shouldn't be escalated. Not unless it was real and she didn't think it was. Jake was so far into game-playing, he was losing his judgement on where the line was crossed. It was wrong to deceive her family. Wrong, wrong, wrong! Especially up close and personal with the whole lot of them!

'Good! Merlina can call her mother and let her know the time of the flight and I'll have one of her brothers meet you at Griffith airport,' her father offered, nailing down the arrangement.

One of her brothers! They'd *all* be eyeing Jake over— the outsider fiancé, a city man who wasn't even Italian.

'That's very kind. Thank you,' Jake said, pouring on the charm.

'Well, I'll leave you two alone then,' her father granted gruffly, not liking the idea at all. 'I did not think you were home, Merlina. You did not answer the telephone. I have arranged to stay with my brother, Georgio, at Glebe.'

'I'll call a taxi for you,' Merlina said, intensely relieved that her father was prepared to leave her and Jake together instead of taking up residence to enforce his moral standards. She'd slid out of Jake's hug and was heading for the telephone in the kitchen when Jake dropped another bomb-shell, halting her in her tracks.

'My car is out the front, Mr Rossi. If you'll give me a few minutes—' his clothes were still on the floor! '—I'll drive you to Glebe myself. It will give us a chance to get to know one another.'

Merlina's stomach curdled at the thought. Had Jake suffered some mad rush of blood to the head?

'Your car…would that be the red Ferrari?' her father inquired.

'Yes, it is,' Jake answered matter-of-factly.

'You have good taste in cars.' A stamp of approval. 'Nothing outclasses the Italians. I have always driven an Alfa, myself. A family sedan these days, but when I was a young man…' He actually smiled at Jake. 'I shall enjoy riding in your Ferrari. Thank you.'

'My pleasure,' Jake rolled out and scooped up his clothes. 'Please excuse me. I won't be long.'

'Take your time,' her father said graciously. After all, he not only had his son-in-law-to-be coming to his party and dancing to his tune, Jake was even providing the Italian music!

Merlina was so stunned by this last development, she was completely robbed of speech as Jake headed for the hall, grinning at her and dropping a kiss on her forehead as he passed her by.

He was having fun.

It *was* a game to him and he was revelling in carrying the ball right into her father's court. He didn't realise that the Rossi playground was hemmed in by rules which had to be respected. Flout them and…panic swirled up again. Her family took some things very, very seriously, and Jake was diving into the deep end without knowing what he was getting into.

Action had to be taken!

She gestured to the sofa as she forced her legs forward, wanting to pick up her own clothes and follow Jake to the bedroom. 'Sit down, Papa. I need to go and have a word with Jake before you leave.'

'Fine-looking man,' he commented, nodding his under-standing of the attraction as he settled himself on the sofa to wait. Then he shook a stern finger at her. 'After we go you must call your mother, Merlina. She will not sleep until she knows all is well with you.'

'I promise I'll do that, Papa.' She'd swept up the offensive clothes. 'If you'll excuse me…'

'Go, go.' He waved her off, adding as she went, 'A fine engagement ring, too. Your mother will be impressed.'

Merlina's heart dropped like a stone. Byron's ring! This was all such a mess! Her head was whirling with frantic thoughts as she hurried to her bedroom. Jake was already dressed, sitting on the bed to pull on his socks and shoes. He glanced up as she backed against the door, pushing it shut behind her to ensure some privacy.

'Are you mad?' she shot at him, trying not to get distracted by the rumpled silk doona, though she was instantly hit by the memory of her writhing in wild abandonment to the intense pleasure he'd given her.

'I thought I was doing really well out there,' he chided, his mouth twitching in amusement.

'You're carrying it too far, Jake,' she cried, lifting her hands in anxious appeal. 'I tried to stop you…'

'I didn't want to be stopped, Merlina.' He bent to tie his shoelaces.

'You don't understand. You're playing with my family. They're not sophisticated city people who'll shrug this off. They'll…'

'I'm not playing.'

'Yes, you are,' she protested fiercely, frustrated by his careless manner.

'No, I'm not.' He stood up, a devil-may-care smile on his face, eyes twinkling wicked pleasure at her as he strode over to slide his arms around her waist and draw her stiffly resistant body against his, re-awakening the carnal desires she had absolutely no control over. 'I've decided to marry you, Merlina Rossi,' he said, cutting through any further protest on her part.

Her heart stopped.

He stroked her cheek, still smiling as she struggled with disbelief. 'Nothing to say?' he teased.

His overbearing confidence, and the angst he had just put her through, sparked a perverse flash of anger. 'I haven't said yes, Jake Devila.'

'You will. I've got you boxed in.'

Then he kissed her, robbing her of any negative response to his triumphant entrapment of her, firing up the passion that made her forget everything else. A savage possessiveness seized her again. She wanted this man. *Take him,* it commanded. *Just take him and don't quibble about the how and the why and what grief the future might bring.*

'Can't keep your father waiting, my little tiger,' he murmured, easing back with far too much control for Merlina's liking.

'Have you stopped to think you're boxing *yourself* in with this tiger?' she retorted, unable to blindly follow what instinct dictated. Marriage meant too much to her.

'We can always get divorced.'

Shock ripped through the irrepressible hope that had been burgeoning from his impulsive decision to marry her. The painful realisation hit that marriage was not a lasting thing to him. His parents were divorced. His grandfather's divorces were legion. It was just a contract he could break when it no longer suited either party. For Jake that would probably be when someone more exciting came along.

That was how he would think. And she hated it. Hated it! If it was only lust and the desire to win this game, revelling in the challenges facing him, enjoying *the fun* of coming out on top against all opposition, what chance did this marriage have? She shouldn't enter into it. She shouldn't go along with him. Yet she couldn't bring herself to say a flat no.

She said another truth instead.

'Divorce is not done in the Rossi family, Jake.'

It was a warning that she needed him to take to heart.

But he didn't.

'Let's see how it goes,' he said blithely. 'I'll pick you up at nine in the morning. We'll go shopping for a ring.'

'You've already showed my father Byron's ring,' she reminded him tersely, frustrated by his carefree attitude.

'Take it off. We'll choose one together.'

'Jake…' It was a cry of torment over the situation he'd manipulated.

'Trust me.' He kissed her again to soothe her distress, then patted her cheek in a tender last salute. 'I'll have your father won over before we get to Glebe.'

'That's not the point,' she cried, desperate for him to understand, take heed.

There was no pause for second thoughts. He was

brimming over with unshakeable confidence in himself. 'We're good together. We're great together. Think about it.' He moved her aside, opened the door, and shot her a last happy grin. 'See you in the morning.'

CHAPTER ELEVEN

BOXED in... Merlina was haunted by those words all night, tossing and turning in between snatches of sleep, which were broken by dreams of being helplessly trapped. This was the punishment for deception, she thought. Jake would never have thought of marriage except for her fake engagement to his grandfather. But what could she do about it?

Her father had been halfway to giving his approval of Jake as a son-in-law before they'd even left together, and no doubt he'd been charmed into proudly accepting him as *family* by the time they'd reached Uncle Georgio's home in Glebe, probably asking him in for a celebratory drink to round off the evening and brag to his brother about Merlina's fiancé.

The call she'd made to her mother had spilled into explanations for her absence—explanations that she knew her father would give, fed to him by Jake. They weren't exactly lies, she'd told herself, though her mother's happy relief that Merlina was finally off the shelf and getting married, and her delight over the family visit tomorrow, had been stomach-churning.

Expectations had been raised.

Expectations had to be met.

Boxed in.

The only person she could talk it over with was Byron—her partner in crime. He was an early riser in the morning so Merlina had time to discuss the situation with him well before Jake arrived at nine o'clock. She telephoned him at seven o'clock, feeling extremely tense and needing support.

Naturally the butler answered her call, immediately expressing concern. 'Is everything all right, Ms Rossi? I did feel that Mr Jake was steamrolling you last night, taking matters into his own hands.'

'He certainly did that, Harold,' she replied with feeling. Amazing really, how comfortable she was with Byron's household. She'd been treated so nicely there, everyone caring about her needs.

'A very compelling young man,' Harold remarked sympathetically.

'Yes,' she agreed. 'And I have to talk to Byron about it, Harold. Is he available?'

'I'm sure Mr Byron will be pleased to hear from you. Just a moment, Ms Rossi. I'll transfer this call to him.'

'Thank you.'

She took a few deep breaths as she waited, trying to reduce her stress level. It was instant balm to her jumpy nerves when she heard the rolling lilt of Byron's charming voice. *He* would understand. He'd understood everything.

'My dear Merlina, have we been successful in corralling the wild one?'

A hysterical little laugh bubbled out. 'If you mean marriage, Jake corralled himself in front of my father last night.'

'Your father?' Said with fascinated interest.

Merlina needed no further prompting to pour out the

whole sequence of events, which had led to her current position as Jake's fiancée in her family's eyes.

'Ah, knight to the rescue,' Byron remarked with relish. 'Good boy! Shows he has inherited my gentlemanly instincts.'

'I don't want Jake to be a gentleman,' she wailed. 'I want him to mean it. Really mean it. And after he involved himself with my family, which believe me, won't take this as a game, he mentioned divorce as a way out in the future. I know that's fairly common in your family, Byron, but it isn't in mine. They're very Italian. *Seriously* Italian.'

'Hmm…' came the sound of serious pondering.

'Take today, for instance,' Merlina ran on, anxiety overflowing. 'He's going to land right in it at the family barbecue—all my married brothers and sisters and their children, not to mention uncles and aunts and grandparents and the new baby—the whole tribe hugging and kissing him in welcome, then cross-examining him about his life.' She heaved a worried sigh.

'None of them divorced, huh?' Byron queried.

'Nor ever likely to be,' rolled emphatically off her tongue.

'You know, Jake might like that. The sense of solid family. Never had it himself. It could rope him right in, Merlina.'

'Or make him run a million miles.'

'No…no…he won't do that. He'll view it as a challenge. Winning them over.'

'A game,' she said despairingly.

'Not necessarily. You're worrying too much, my dear. Jake would not have brought up marriage if it wasn't on his mind.'

'Because you—we—put it there, Byron.'

'A seed doesn't grow if it hasn't been planted in ground that suits it. You and he suit each other very well. That is very, very obvious to me.'

We're good together. We're great together.

Her heart thumped with unquenchable hope as she remembered Jake's words.

'Give it a chance,' Byron advised. 'See how it goes.'

Precisely what Jake had said.

Was she worrying too much?

'You want this, Merlina,' Byron reminded her. 'You wouldn't have played the game with me if you hadn't wanted to bring Jake to heel. He's there now because he wants to be there. Let him be embraced by your family. Go with the flow. Be happy, my dear. A man likes his woman to be happy.'

Difficult to be happy when she felt so agitated, yet Byron was right. She had wanted this outcome, except it had happened upon her so fast, she couldn't bring herself to trust it, especially when divorce had been mentioned in virtually the same breath as marriage.

'Okay, I'll go with the flow today and see how it pans out,' she said, screwing herself to the sticking point.

'Good girl! Nothing ventured, nothing gained. Got to be in there playing the game,' Byron cheerfully chanted.

Which brought home to her how very alike grandfather and grandson were. She was probably off her head to be asking advice from Byron. On the other hand, he had given her an insight into where Jake was coming from. People from broken homes didn't believe in lasting promises. That didn't mean they didn't want a commitment to stay solid. Maybe—just maybe—she could work it so the game with Jake never ended.

'Thank you, Byron,' she said gratefully. 'You've just bolstered me up for the next round.'

'Bravo! And the best of luck to you, my dear.'

'I'll keep your diamond ring safe until I see you again,' she promised.

'Wear Jake's with pride, Merlina. He'd like that.'

'Will do. 'Bye for now.'

'Happy days!'

She was smiling as she put the telephone receiver down. *Happy days*...probably a fool's paradise but why not enjoy what Jake gave her while she could, anyway? Her body clenched at the memory of last night's sexual pleasure. He was such a great lover and it had felt like being loved—beautifully, wonderfully loved. If he wanted their relationship to last, she had to give it a chance!

There was a happy spring in her step as she raced off to her bedroom to decide on what to wear this morning. Definitely classy elegance for the kind of jewellery shop Jake would take her to if he was intent on putting just as flashy a ring as his grandfather's on her finger.

She chose one of her new purchases; a form-fitting red dress, printed with abstract splashes of black and white, featuring a wide square neckline, little cap sleeves and a wide woven belt in white. It was simple but quite striking, especially teamed with high-heeled white sandals and a white clutch bag. Class, she had worked out, could be achieved by meticulous attention to detail.

On this principle, she applied a matching red varnish to her toenails and fingernails, took immense care with her make-up, and as a final touch, attached long dangly vintage gold earrings to her lobes. To her mind, these went with the vintage style gold watch—a twenty-first birthday gift from her grandmother—which was the only other jewel-lery she wore, having hidden Byron's ring at the bottom of an open bag of peas in the freezer.

The doorbell rang at five minutes to nine. No nervous waiting around for Jake to come, for which she was in-tensely grateful. Her heart was fluttering wildly enough as it was. She opened the door to find him superbly dressed in a pin-striped grey suit, white shirt, gold silk tie, and looking more dashingly handsome than ever, especially when he smiled at her, his dark eyes dancing with pleasure in her appearance.

'Wow! When you make up your mind to sock it to me, Merlina, you sure sock it to me. Red is definitely your colour.'

She was instantly reminded of the red rose bikini. Boldness had served her well as the blonde bimbo from the birthday cake, so she impulsively struck a flaunting pose, jutting out one hip and planting her hands on her tightly belted waist. 'Thought I'd better wear it since you're into rescuing scarlet women from damnation,' she flipped at him, lowering her eyelashes for a sizzling veiled look.

He laughed, and with a bold move of his own, scooped her back into the hall, closed the door behind them and wrapped her in a very possessive embrace. 'So, the real Merlina emerges in a full frontal assault,' he purred like a big cat presented with a delicious dinner. He grinned from ear to ear as he teasingly added, 'Am I man enough for her?'

She arched an eyebrow. 'Depends on whether you got through last night unscathed by my father.'

'Passed with flying colours,' he declared with relish. 'Bring on any challenge you like. I'm up for it.'

'Mmm…' In sheer giddy delight at feeling his erection against her stomach, knowing that seeing her had aroused it and madly wanting to stoke his desire for her even further, she brazenly rubbed her lower body against his, smiling as she said, 'Up for something else, too.'

His answering smile was positively wicked. 'The only question is…are you? Right this minute!'

He started walking her backwards, his thighs pushing hers, steering her across the living room towards the dining table, which was set beside the window. 'Where are you taking me?' she asked, startled by the instant reaction she'd triggered and barely finding breath enough to speak. Her pulse was galloping. Excitement was rushing through her like a freight train.

'I'd take you anywhere, Merlina Rossi,' he answered, his eyes smouldering with sexual intent as he propped her against the edge of the table and started gathering up her skirt.

'Not tonight in my parents' home, you won't,' she flashed at him, momentarily panicking at the thought. 'We'll be given separate bedrooms. And you have to respect that, Jake.'

'Okay. How about now?'

His thumbs were already hooked on the waistband of her panties, ready to pull them down, but he paused teasingly, confident of her consent but also wanting to make her say it out loud.

'Do we have time?' she posed coquettishly.

He laughed. 'For this we make time.'

'Fine by me,' she admitted, dying to have him inside her again and exhilarated that he wanted to be there.

She stepped out of the panties as he drew them down. No pantihose today. She'd left her legs bare, wanting her red toenails to show against the white sandals. Which he left on. With her skirt hitched up around her hips, he sat her on the table and moved between her legs, clearly intent on quick action. Only essential undressing this morning.

'Maybe you'd better tell me our schedule for today,' she said, watching him unzip, wanting to see what she'd already felt, her inner muscles already pulsing with the anticipation of being stroked and pleasured, wanting to squeeze her own possession of him, feel him fill her so deeply she couldn't think of anything to worry about.

He shot her his devil-may-care grin. 'You first.' He extracted a condom from his wallet and proceeded to roll it on.

Won't have to use that when we're married, Merlina thought, which instantly reminded her... *What about children?* Her heart jiggled uncertainly. Would Jake want to be a father?

'Then off we go to buy a ring,' he said, shooting her another grin. 'For a scarlet woman, I think we should choose a ruby. It can be set with diamonds but we should definitely have a red-blooded ruby at the centre.'

Laughter gurgled from her throat. Jake Devila was a terrible playboy but she loved him. Loved everything about him. 'It won't look like the other one,' she pointed out.

'Which I hope you've taken off.' He whipped her hand down from around his neck to check. 'Ah!' he said with satisfaction.

'I put it in a safe place,' she rattled out.

'This place is mine.' He stunned her by drawing her ring finger into his mouth, sucking on it as his eyes glittered his own rampant desire to possess her.

It took a few moments to catch her breath enough to say, 'My father will notice the difference.'

He released her finger and answered with his usual arrogant confidence. 'Your father thinks I surprised you with that one. You didn't really like it so today we chose one together. How's that?'

He'd slid between her thighs, seeking entry, and was teasingly poised to push forward. 'Fine!' she approved, finding it extremely erotic to be carrying on a conversation while everything within her was thumping a wild welcome to the sexual connection with him. 'What's next?' she asked, feeling wickedly provocative.

'Right now I want to feel your flesh ringing mine,' he said, forging the deeply intimate link, then lowering her back onto the table as she wound her legs around his hips, instinctively compelling the fulfilment of her need for him. 'My scarlet woman,' he murmured with relish as his hands glided over the curves of her breasts, still trapped inside the bodice of her dress.

She smiled, loving the possessive pleasure in his voice, revelling in the desire that couldn't wait. He drove himself in hard, his body slamming against her and she arched up, squeezing him in blissful joy. A wild savagery leapt into his eyes. He leaned over and kissed her, his tongue driving into her mouth, plunging rhythmically to assert complete ownership, hunting for sexual domination which she readily conceded, revelling in the intense physical passion, the climactic urgency of it, moving together, reaching for the same ecstatic release, a fusing frenzy of explosive excitement that peaked exultantly and floated into sweet endearments as he cuddled her close, gruffly whispering, 'My gorgeous girl…you are unbelievable…so beautiful…awesome…'

She ran her fingers through his hair, adoring every touch of him. 'So are you,' she whispered back.

He lifted his head, brushing his lips over hers. 'What am I going to do with you?' It sounded as though she was a puzzle to which he had no reference points for resolving.

'You said you were going to marry me,' she reminded him.

He laughed, his eyes twinkling at hers. 'That's a definite start.'

A start.

But would there be a finish line?

Merlina fiercely clamped down on this negative train of thought. Jake wanted to marry her. Maybe it would work out perfectly. Not to take the chance was unthinkable.

'We go now and buy the ring,' he ran on. 'Then since I feel on top of the world, we'll have a celebratory lunch at Level 21 and enjoy overlooking Sydney. After which we'll catch our two-thirty flight to Griffith…'

'You've booked it?'

'Mmm…' He flashed his wicked grin. 'And since we're doomed to separate bedrooms in your family home, maybe you can take me for a walk in the vineyard your father told me about. Before we retire for the night.'

The instant thrill at this suggestion told Merlina that sex with Jake was already highly addictive and she couldn't possibly turn her back on it at this juncture. Whatever the future brought, she would never regret having known the best of Jake Devila.

'There's no such thing as privacy anywhere near my family, Jake,' she warned ruefully. 'You'll be swamped by them this evening.'

'I have you as my lifeboat.'

'Uh-uh.' She shook her head. 'You'll lose respect if you look to me for rescue. It's sink or swim for you.'

'I'm a natural born survivor,' he claimed, not the slightest dint in his confidence.

But it was a different game, Merlina thought, and the rules would be foreign to him. 'Just take it easy,' she advised seriously. 'Don't try too hard.' She wanted her family to like him, to accept him into their fold.

He gently stroked the worry lines from her forehead. 'I've got your father onside,' he reminded her. 'I promise you, it won't be a problem, Merlina. Don't fret over it.'

She couldn't help it. Jake was into winning but laying a solid foundation with her family required genuine responses that struck harmonious chords. If that didn't happen…well, she did have the choice of going it alone with him. Though even contemplating that path brought a scary sense of loss. She might have chosen to live apart from her family most of the time but she wanted them there for her. As they'd always been.

'Have you packed a bag ready to go?' he asked.

'Yes. It's in my bedroom.'

'Good. Mine's in the car.' He sat her up on the table and kissed her again, a very fresh reminder of what they'd just experienced together, ending in a sigh of resignation over the time factor. 'Guess we'd better move, tidy up and head into the city.'

'Guess we'd better,' she agreed, echoing his sigh.

He smiled. 'No argument from you this morning?'

She cocked her head considering, giving him a look that telegraphed he was flirting with danger as she replied, 'Not until you do something I don't like.'

He laughed and set her down on her feet, hugging her close for a few more moments of sweet togetherness. 'I promise not to be a bad boy in front of your family. Okay?'

'I live in hope that you can keep that promise,' she said with dry irony, knowing that any challenge was meat and drink to Jake.

'Watch me,' he threw back at her, not the least bit intimidated by the prospect of being measured as an appropriate husband.

Maybe their relationship would thrive if she could just keep throwing out challenges, Merlina thought, as she was scooped along with him *to get tidy.*

But there was still the burning issue of parenthood.

How would he respond to Mario and Gina's new baby?

She really would have to watch Jake.

Actions were much more telling than words.

CHAPTER TWELVE

JAKE had time for some private reflection as he waited for Merlina to emerge from the ladies' room at the airport. She'd insisted on their changing clothes before boarding their flight to Griffith and he had already swapped his suit for jeans and a green sports shirt—suitable for any barbecue—and was wondering what kind of outfit she would choose for the family party.

He'd learnt a great deal about the real Merlina in the past twenty-four hours, one revelation after another. She'd caught his interest and intrigued him from their very first meeting, but knowing her far more intimately now, being with her, was exhilarating on every level. His proposal of marriage had been impulsive but he didn't regret it. In fact, it gave him immense satisfaction to see *his* ring on Merlina's finger.

It was weird in a way, since he hadn't given marriage a thought until last night. He'd always figured it was not worth the trouble; all the fuss of a showcase wedding, a few years of finding out and suffering through incompatibilities, then paying for the mistake in the divorce court.

But he'd stepped up to the plate for Merlina without a second's hesitation. What's more, he felt really good about it. The trick now was to make her feel good about it. She didn't yet. She'd kept glancing at the ruby and diamond ring all through lunch as though she couldn't really believe it was there, and she was uptight about this meeting with her family, despite the assurances he'd given her about being on his best behaviour.

He had more or less trapped her into this situation and she probably had a lot of doubts about marrying a man she viewed as a playboy. It was true enough that he made a game of life—best way to deal with it, in his opinion—but that didn't mean he couldn't stick at something if he wanted to. If he had good reason to.

The *good reason* came sailing out of the ladies' room dressed in figure-hugging white slacks and a red silky top with an open white collar—sporty and sexy. The tense look on her face eased into a smile of relief as she took in his changed appearance. Jake felt no relief at all. Just the sight of her aroused him again and he didn't know how he was going to contain this rampant desire until tomorrow. Hopefully her family would provide many distractions.

'Am I more acceptable now?' he asked quizzically.

Her smile took on a slight wince. 'You did look very *city* in your suit.'

'So we're into images again, are we?' he teased.

Amazingly she blushed and he caught a glimpse of anxious vulnerability in her eyes as she tried to explain. 'We are stepping into their world, Jake. I know you don't fit…won't fit…'

'Hey!' He stepped forward and drew her into his embrace. 'I'm happy to go with the flow wherever it takes me, Merlina. And I'm perfectly comfortable in this gear, as you very well know. It's what I wear to work.'

'Yes. Yes, it is.' The reminder relaxed her.

Trying to lighten her mood further, he said, 'You know what your problem is? You didn't plan this yourself so you don't have every detail under your control. But sometimes, my bride-to-be, you have to wing it.'

She laughed somewhat nervously. 'Believe me, I'm winging it, Jake.'

'Then come fly with me,' he tossed back at her, smiling to win her compliance and confidence as he retained one arm around her waist and turned her to walk with him to the departure lounge.

Jake had no concern whatsoever over *fitting*. It was simply a matter of adapting to the circumstances and blending with the environment. He'd been doing it most of his life, having learnt the *sink or swim* principle at a very early age. His parents' divorce had messed him around for a while but it had forged a strong sense of independence from how they carried on. In fact, the game of *survival of the fittest* had always appealed to his competitive nature and he was not about to lose today.

Merlina fell into step with him, biting back the fear that flying with Jake Devila might end in crashing and burning. They rolled their repacked overnight bags along with them to stow in the lockers above their seats on the plane. No waiting for baggage at the other end of the flight. She'd telephoned her mother to give the time of their arrival and had been told that two of her brothers, Danny who was thirty-four, and Joe, thirty-three, would meet them and bring them home.

She knew both of them would have regarded Jake as a city slicker in his classy suit. First impressions were important.

Though Jake was right about images. Of course he could *seem* to fit in. And no doubt he would *work* at fitting in. He was very skilled at handling people. But what would he be thinking and feeling behind the easy charm he would apply?

She knew he wanted her.

And meant to have her as long as the wanting lasted.

Apart from lust and the will to win, Jake's feelings were a mystery to her and she needed to know them before they got married. As much as she yearned to be with Jake, she couldn't really wing marriage. It was too important. A contract for life. Involving children.

She had to watch him.

Had to see.

Not be blinded by her own feelings for him—the need to hold on which was growing stronger by the minute.

Jake used the flight time to pump Merlina for all the names and relationships of the family members who would be attending the party, sorting them out in his mind, making associations and placing them in his memory bank. It was like preparing for a business meeting. The numbers were bigger for this meeting, but by mentally reciting the connections over and over, he felt he had them pegged well enough to facilitate introductions and subsequent conversations.

However, he wasn't prepared for the sheer exuberance of Danny's and Joe's welcome; two big burly men picking Merlina up, swinging her around, hugging and kissing with real affection, clapping him on the back, shaking his hand with both of theirs, shooting happy comments at them.

'Hey, Merlina! Got yourself a man at last!'

'Good man, Jake! Thought we'd never get Miss Independence hitched up with anyone.'

'Mamma's in seventh heaven what with a birth and a wedding to celebrate.'

'Going to have us a great party tonight!'

The warmth of their uninhibited joy swirled around Jake, tapping into hollow places in his soul and making him feel strangely uneasy. He wasn't used to such genuine bonhomie. It wasn't practised charm. It came from the heart. His own smile felt oddly false in comparison to their delighted grins.

An animated conversation was carried on as the two brothers escorted them out of the airport terminal and to a four-wheel-drive Land Rover in the car-park. Once they were settled in the vehicle and on their way to the Rossi vineyard, more personal attention was focussed on Jake.

'So you were Merlina's boss,' Danny started. 'Tell us about your business, Jake.'

He explained what Signature Sounds entailed. Aware that some European ringtone companies had earned a bad reputation for hooking in kids and signing them up for contracts that exploited them, Jake took care to let Merlina's family know that his sales were straightforward, no trickery involved. Customers got only what they wanted and were prepared to pay for and anyone under eighteen had to have a parent countersign a contract.

Both Danny and Joe owned cell-phones and were computer literate—technology that no business could do without in today's world—but they expressed amazement at what Jake sold.

'You mean people actually pay to replace the usual beeping with some tra-la-la as a call signal on their cell-phone?'

'It personalises communication,' Jake pointed out.

'What's wrong with giving your name?'

'Nothing. This is a novelty. It amuses people.'

'Probably drives them mad, too.'

'In that event it gets a very quick response.'

'Yeah, right! Shut the damned thing off.'

'Noise pollution.'

'Not necessarily,' Jake corrected, feeling uncharacteristically defensive. 'We market a broad range of sounds, some very pleasant to the ear. More so than beeping.'

'And you've built a business out of this?'

The sense that they thought it was stupid trivia was very strong. Jake had never questioned the value of what he did. He'd thought the idea was marketable and he'd been proven right. Financially it had been a huge success, which he naturally enjoyed. But what he sold had no intrinsic worth. It was ephemeral stuff. Somehow that realisation knocked the shine off his pride in his achievement.

'The most popular sounds Jake has marketed have made millions of sales worldwide,' Merlina quietly supplied.

'You're kidding!'

'No. Lots of people get a buzz out of using them,' she stated matter-of-factly. 'It gives them a sense of individuality, expressing something about themselves. Don't knock it just because you've never thought of doing it.'

She was defending him.

Or attacking her brothers for being narrow-minded.

Was that why she had left here and come to the city, seeking a broader life?

'Didn't mean to knock it, Jake,' Danny said apologetically. 'If it works for you, that's fine.'

'Guess we find it a strange world out there,' Joe remarked ruefully.

'A very diverse world,' Jake put in, feeling better about his business and giving Merlina's hand an appreciative squeeze for her support.

They'd headed away from the town of Griffith, straight into the countryside from the airport, and the brothers now started to point out the vineyards belonging to the family, informing Jake of the different types of grapes they cultivated and what wines they made.

Their pride in the property they owned and in what they produced set off another wave of discomfort in Jake. Merlina was right. He'd stepped into a different world with these people—a more solid, tangible, tactile world—and he was suddenly envious of the belonging they obviously felt to this place.

They'd been born here, raised here, worked here and would probably die here. A narrow existence, Jake told himself, but they exuded a contentment he hadn't experienced himself. He'd never become attached to a place. His mother had liked changing houses. The longest he'd stayed anywhere was at boarding school, which had been tolerable enough, though not a home from home. His grandfather's mansion at Vaucluse had been the one constant in his life, but visiting was not the same as belonging. Even the penthouse apartment he now owned had no emotional tug on him.

'Here we are!' Joe announced as the Land Rover was turned towards a gate, which was inhabited by a tribe of children hanging off its cross-bars. Two dogs—a Labrador and a boxer—were prancing around behind them, barking their heads off. Joe leaned out the window to yell, 'Open up, you kids.'

A boy jumped down to push the gate open while the rest stayed on for the ride, waving and shouting excitedly.

'Hey, Merlina, we've got a new baby brother.'

'Merlina, we want to see your boyfriend.'

'He's her fiancé, not her boyfriend.'

'I want to meet him first.'

'No, me, me, me.'

'Merlina, how about walking down to the house with us?'

A loud chorus of 'Yeahs,' had Joe stopping the Land Rover and turning his head towards the back seat to ask, 'Do you want to walk from here?'

Merlina looked to Jake.

'Wouldn't want to disappoint them. Let's go,' he said, opening his door, ready to alight.

By the time he rounded the vehicle, Merlina was already out and the mob of children was surging forward to greet and meet, the dogs racing up to sniff and be patted.

Jake had never owned a dog—no pet of any kind—and he wondered what it might have been like to be greeted every day with tail-wagging affection. It would surely have taken away some of the loneliness of his boyhood. These children were lucky, having a big, close-knit family, mixing together with natural ease, having a sense of permanence in their environment which allowed for pets to live with them.

Joe and Danny drove on, having been relieved of escort duty, and Jake enjoyed the new company; the boys' perky questions, the coy shyness of the little girls, the teasing good humour that flashed around all of them. It was obvious that Merlina was a favourite with her nieces and nephews. He noticed she wasn't bored by them. They weren't a nuisance to her. And she didn't talk down to them, treating everything they said to her with natural interest, drawing them out and giving responses that gave them pleasure or made them laugh.

It struck Jake that she would be a good mother, which jolted him into remembering she wanted children of her own. That was part of the marriage deal for her and he hadn't given it a thought. He started studying the children milling around him, trying to imagine himself as a father. Was it a role he wanted to play?

His own father had absconded to Europe after his mother had divorced him and Jake hadn't seen him since. He'd envied the kids at school who had dads come to watch their sporting events. A father should be there, Jake thought, taking an interest, giving encouragement and approval. No one should have children unless they were prepared to do that. Which meant giving a lot of time to them.

A little girl—was it three-year-old Rosa?—tugged at his jeans to gain his attention, looking up at him with big, imploring eyes. 'My legs are tired,' she said woefully. 'Will you carry me on your shoulders, Jake?'

'I sure will.' He hoisted her up and she dug her fingers into his hair to hold on. He'd never carried a child like this but she obviously trusted him to do it right and knew how to balance herself. Her father must have made her feel confident about it.

'If you're so tired, Rosa, you won't be able to play soccer after dinner,' one of the boys remarked.

'Oh, yes I will,' she said with emphatic determination. 'I just need a little rest, that's all.'

'You never score a goal anyway,' he tossed back.

'I'm going to have Jake on my side tonight,' she retaliated. 'He won't let you take the ball off me.'

'I think you've just been elected Rosa's champion,' Merlina said, giving him a rueful smile.

He raised his eyebrows in an appeal for help. 'What does that mean?'

Everyone rushed in to explain. Poppa had set up a junior soccer field for them behind the house. The adults could play but they were only allowed to trap and pass the soccer ball on to the children, not score a goal. They always had a game after a family barbecue. The two smallest children picked their teams, so Rosa was one captain and four-year-old Genarro was the other. The women didn't play. They sat on the veranda and cheered on the teams.

'A bit of discrimination here?' Jake tilted at Merlina.

She rolled her eyes. 'You can't beat family tradition.'

'You played when you were a kid?'

'I have the record for most goals scored by a girl.'

He laughed. 'I bet you were a tiger on the field.'

'It was a challenge.'

'And you took it on in your usual tenacious manner, refusing to be defeated.'

She gave him an ironic look. 'You know me too well.'

'No. But I'm getting there.'

Like learning about where she'd come from; this huge family community, which actually had traditions passed down from generation to generation, a world with different values to those he was familiar with. He'd moved himself past the sense of having been cheated of a family life when he was a boy, yet he was feeling it again now, very strongly, so strongly it stirred a long-suppressed anger at the parental neglect that had left him deprived of all this.

Merlina was right.

He didn't fit.

All his bearings ran along different tracks.

But something in him longed to fit.

Being here was like looking over a fence at what should have been. It hurt in ways he hadn't anticipated. The fence was uncrossable. Or was it? He couldn't change his past but he could determine his future. Maybe, if he had children with Merlina, he could climb over to the other side, sharing it with them.

He turned his gaze to the big sprawling house they were approaching. It was a country house, wide verandas running all around it, trees providing shade and handy branches for children to climb. Garden beds were a profusion of colour with petunias and geraniums mixed in with the greenery of shrubs. It was not a show-place. It looked very much lived in—a real family home.

To one side of it was a huge shed with a row of vehicles parked in front of it; pick-up trucks, four-wheel drives, station wagons, a couple of sedans, nothing that screamed status class. It wasn't for a lack of money, Jake thought. Properties like this were probably worth a fortune. Any other symbols of prosperity were simply irrelevant. These people weren't out to impress. They were who they were— the Rossi family.

Merlina's family.

Joe and Danny were leaning on the veranda railing near the front door, watching their approach. They were joined by another brother.

'That's Mario, the father of the new baby,' Merlina informed him.

Her father emerged from the house, standing at the top of the front steps to welcome them. 'All you children scoot off and play now,' he commanded. 'I'll be taking Jake and Merlina in to Nonna.'

He was instantly obeyed. No back-chat. Jake lifted

Rosa down from his shoulders. The little girl thanked him and skipped off after the others, her legs in good working order again.

'I see my daughter has you twined around her finger already, Jake,' Danny commented with a wide grin.

Angelo Rossi laughed as he grasped Jake's hand in greeting. 'Our little Rosa is a cute one. But wait until you see my new grandson. You'll be wanting a boy just like him.'

'Papa, we're not even married yet,' Merlina protested.

'So? What is marriage without children? The two of you will make beautiful bambinos.'

It was expected of him, and not just by Merlina, Jake thought. Was he up for it? Seriously? This whole family thing was part and parcel of marrying her. She had warned him and he could feel her tension mounting as he was introduced to Mario and did his best to warmly congratulate him on his new son.

Angelo steered him inside and down a long hallway to a huge kitchen at the end of it—the biggest kitchen Jake had ever seen with copper pots and pans hanging everywhere and a long table in the centre of it, laden with bowls of salads and baskets of bread. The room seemed crowded with women—big women—all of them looking him over with avid interest.

One of them clapped her hands in delighted approval, opened her arms wide and swooped on him, hugging him to her very ample bosom and kissing him effusively on both cheeks.

'My wife, Maria,' Angelo said proudly, adding, 'Merlina's mother,' for good measure.

'You are so welcome!' Maria cried. 'So very welcome! I despaired of Merlina ever marrying anyone and you...'

'Oh, Mamma,' Merlina groaned.

Maria ignored her, patting his cheeks. 'Such a handsome man…'

'You have a beautiful daughter,' Jake found wits enough to say.

She released him to clap her hands again. 'This is so exciting!'

Then recollecting herself she turned to the other women, literally presenting him for more hugs and kisses as he was introduced to Merlina's aunts, sisters and sisters-in-law. Being welcomed into the bosom of this family took on a very physical meaning. He'd got into the way of it by the last introduction and quite happily succumbed to be being squashed into soft female flesh. It felt surprisingly good, a far cry from the air-kisses of the social set in Sydney.

Gina, the new mother, took him over to a bassinet to show off her baby son. 'He's asleep now but I'll let you hold him later when he wakes up,' she offered as though he would naturally want to.

Jake wasn't at all sure about that. It was the smallest human being he had ever seen, but its tiny face was sort of endearing, framed as it was by a mass of spiky black hair. 'I can see he's going to have lots of personality,' was the best comment he could come up with.

It seemed to please Gina and the other women laughed their approval. He glanced at Merlina and caught a drowning look of despair in her eyes. It hit him instantly that she didn't believe his marriage proposal would survive having her family's expectations pressed upon him. She was twisting his ring around her finger in agitation, as though already thinking of taking it off.

He reacted without a second thought, moving quickly

to hug her to his side, stopping the fretting movement by taking her left hand and holding it out for the women to see the ruby and diamond ring. 'Merlina is not used to wearing this yet. I want you to tell her how great it looks on her finger so she won't feel nervous about it,' he said, spreading an appealing smile to all of them.

'Oh, Merlina! It is beautiful!' her mother cried, rushing forward for a closer examination.

Angelo laughed and said, 'Leave Merlina to the women, Jake. It is time we men fired up the barbecue to cook the children's dinner.'

'Yes, yes, the meat is on the tray ready for you, Angelo,' Maria tossed at him. 'Off you both go.'

No choice, Jake realised.

He had to do what was expected of him.

While he hadn't thought through all that a marriage with Merlina Rossi would encompass, he knew one thing for certain.

He didn't want to let her out of his life.

Not at this point.

Possibly not ever.

She was beginning to represent all the good things he'd missed out on.

CHAPTER THIRTEEN

MERLINA watched Jake accompany her father out of the kitchen, stunned that he had just reinforced their engagement by focussing her family's attention on the ring, which was being volubly admired even as she struggled to understand his action.

Why had he done it?

She knew Danny and Joe had rubbed him up the wrong way with their comments on his business, belittling it, then carrying on about their own. She'd sensed his irritation, his mental withdrawal, though he'd been polite enough to cover it up, smoothly inquiring about the wine-making process, pretending to be impressed by *their* export figures.

Being swamped by the children hadn't seemed to bother him. The idea of the soccer game tradition had definitely twigged amusement, but she'd almost died on the spot when her father had charged in about having *bambinos*. While there could be no escaping the subject—she did want to be a mother—to have it shoved point-blank in Jake's face…she'd imagined the idea of marriage with her moving straight into a death spiral.

Then his shoulders had stiffened as her mother enveloped him in one of her compelling hugs, invading his

personal space like a runaway train. Just prior to that he'd
been looking around the women in the kitchen, probably
comparing them negatively to the sleek sophisticated
women he was used to. She could almost hear the questions in his mind—

*Would Merlina blow out to super size in a few years' time?
Is this what happened when Italian women had children?*

Of course, everyone had to get in on the hug/kiss act and
Jake had managed to take the poker out of his spine. For a
man who'd always preferred skinny women, he had stuck
in there accepting the embraces of the plumper variety
with a fair show of appreciating their generous welcome,
for which Merlina was extremely grateful. Indeed, he
hadn't put a foot wrong, despite being plunged into alien
territory.

But what he *thought* was something else entirely and
Merlina acutely felt the strain of wondering what was going
on in his mind. And heart. Especially when Gina had put
him in the position of having to admire her new son. Coming
on top of the *bambino* comment from her father, Jake's
head must have been spinning with the obligations and re-
sponsibilities attached to marrying into the Rossi family.

It was probably the first time in his life he'd wanted to
escape from a roomful of women, though being with the
men en masse would undoubtedly present other awkward
moments. Had he ever been expected to help cook a
barbecue in his entire playboy life? To Merlina's mind it was
a case of jumping out of the frying pan, straight into the fire.

And it wasn't so good for her in the frying pan area,
either, having to smile happily while showing off the ruby
and diamond ring and field a plethora of questions about
Jake and their engagement. She couldn't feel comfortable

about it. Everything had happened too fast, and she suspected Jake had leapt onto this marriage merry-go-round without seeing it as a serious step to take.

In the midst of this emotional turmoil, Sylvana suggested she help her arrange the platters of antipasta, obviously wanting to have her own personal curiosity satisfied. The laser treatment on her eyes had been successful. She wasn't wearing glasses any more. Which made the inquisitive interest beamed at Merlina far too bright for comfort.

'Now I know why you cut your hair and wore such revealing clothes,' she archly remarked.

'That went with the job, Sylvana.'

Which reminded her that looking for a new job had gone right out of her head and some decisions about her future had to be made very soon.

'Oh, come on!' Sylvana chided. 'A gorgeous man like that! I bet you fell in love with him on the spot and would have done anything to please him.'

She was about to say, *It wasn't like that,* then swallowed the words, realising there was more than a grain of truth in them. 'Perhaps you're right. I was attracted to him from the start.'

'Who wouldn't be? And having the job as his personal assistant certainly gave you an *in*. Nothing like constant proximity for catching a guy's interest,' Sylvana said smugly.

It was more her departure from the job that had triggered Jake's pursuit of her. Plus his furious frustration over her subsequent attachment to his grandfather. He'd been goaded into chasing after her, and she'd done the goading out of her own frustration with him. They'd both wanted to win, but they should both take a long hard look at what winning meant in case the end result was a terrible mistake.

'When are you going to get married?' Sylvana pressed.

'I don't know. We haven't talked about dates yet.'

'Mamma will want to know. You can't not have the wedding here.'

Irritated by her sister's pushiness, Merlina burst out, 'Stop laying down the law to me. I won't be boxed in, Sylvana. This is my life. And Jake's. We'll marry wherever we want to.'

Shock ran around the kitchen. Everyone stopped doing what they were doing to stare at her—the rebel who had left the nest, rather than fit in like the rest of them.

'Merlina…' her mother started, looking apprehensively at her wayward daughter.

'Mamma, I'm not even sure I do want to marry him,' she cried, giving vent to her bottled up anxiety.

Her mother frowned. 'But you love him, don't you?'

'That's not the point!'

'You have been a career woman too long, Merlina. You are nervous about being a wife.'

She clutched at that straw, feeling she was drowning in this whole situation. 'Yes. Yes, I am.'

Her mother nodded knowingly. 'This is why Jake was concerned about your keeping his ring.'

'I just don't know, Mamma. He…he surprised me with it.'

'He is a good man, Merlina. Your father likes him. Give it time. We will not rush you into planning.'

Relief poured through her. 'Thanks, Mamma. I'm not ready for planning.'

'Always you think too much, Merlina. With Jake you should go with your heart.'

There was a chorus of fervent agreement around the kitchen. Merlina was inundated with the joys of being a wife and mother, the comfort of having a partner to share everything with, etc etc etc. It was a constant eulogy to marriage, which only stopped when all the prepared food was taken out to the long tressle table on the back veranda and there was nothing more to do until the meat was cooked.

Merlina tried to take her mother's advice about not thinking too much. However, she did not regret her outburst in the kitchen. At least the family was now warned that the engagement might not last, and Jake would not be subjected to a whole lot of plans about the wedding. Indeed her mother must have had a private word to her father about their unmarried daughter's *nerves*.

He was relatively subdued over dinner, and when it came time for the toasts to the new baby and the newly engaged couple with prized wine from a very good vintage year, he did not rave on about looking forward to more *bambinos*, nor did he break into grandiose suggestions for setting out marquees on the soccer field for the wedding reception.

Jake was favoured with much kindly attention.

Merlina was treated warily.

Apparently her father did not want his runaway daughter to become a runaway bride.

To his credit, Jake had settled into a good-humoured groove; smiling, laughing, happily joining in general conversations, listening attentively to whatever her family had to say. Underneath the table his thigh pressed against hers, silently communicating the desire for more intimacy with her. She ached for more intimacy with him and knew she didn't want to give it up, but if a proper marriage was not to his taste, then she really should break up with him.

After dinner, Rosa and Genarro picked their soccer

teams, and off they all trotted to occupy the field and get the game under way. The score was three all in the second half when Jake trapped the ball on the wing and passed it to Rosa who was waiting hopefully in a striking position near the other team's goal. Two of the boys raced to take it off her but Jake intercepted both of them, hoisting them up against his shoulders as they struggled to get away.

It gave Rosa time to dribble the ball forward and kick it past the oncoming goalie into the corner of the net. In her absolute glee at scoring, she pulled her T-shirt up over her head, held her arms high and ran screaming around the sideline as though she'd just won The World Cup. Everyone collapsed in laughter and the game was abandoned, the decision being made that nothing could top that. Jake, Rosa's hero, carried her off the field, triumphantly seated on his shoulders.

'I'm always going to have you on my team, Jake,' Rosa declared.

Always was another big word, Merlina thought.

'I'll try to be here for you, Rosa, but I might not get to every family barbecue,' Jake replied. 'Sydney is a long way away.'

A whole world away.

And Jake had to be as conscious of it as Merlina was, but he grinned at her and said, 'That was fun,' as though he really meant it.

She desperately wanted to get him to herself for a while, time alone together so he would not have to keep up the appearance of enjoying himself with her family. If this was simply a game he was playing, she needed to know. She couldn't bear the confusion much longer. Dealing with the truth would be infinitely better, even if it was a painful truth.

Since it was a school day tomorrow, the party broke up relatively early so the children could still get a good night's sleep. The long summer's day was over, twilight darkening the sky to purple. Everyone pitched in to get the cleaning up done before they left. Farewells were not lingered over though no one neglected to express pleasure in meeting Jake and wishing him and Merlina much happiness together. Her face grew stiff from the effort of holding a smile. She wondered if Jake was wishing them gone as much as she was.

Ironically enough, her mother decided to play Cupid. 'Why don't you take Jake for a stroll down the wisteria walk to the orchard while there's still light enough to see, Merlina?' she said as they stood on the front veranda, waving off the last car to leave.

Surprisingly her father promoted the idea. 'The wisteria is no longer in bloom,' he informed Jake. 'But it's still a pretty walk. You won't have a chance in the morning. Have to be at the airport half an hour before your six-forty-five flight.'

Jake hooked her arm around his. 'Let's go,' he said eagerly, his eyes lighting up at the opportunity to do more than stroll.

'We won't wait up for you, Merlina,' her mother hastened to say. 'Jake, you know where your room is?'

'Yes, thank you. Danny showed me earlier.'

'Then sleep well, both of you.'

'Thanks, Mamma,' Merlina chimed in quickly. 'Good night. You, too, Papa.'

'Oh, to be young again, eh, Maria?' her father said, hugging her mother as they headed back into the house.

'You think you are still young, Angelo,' she tossed back with arch meaning.

Jake chuckled over this sexual allusion as she steered him around the veranda to the south side which faced the orchard. 'How old *is* your father?' he asked, still amused by the exchange between her parents.

'Sixty-four.'

Another little laugh. 'Pop thinks he's still young at eighty.'

The mention of his grandfather stirred a hornet's nest in Merlina's brain and she was instantly stung into saying, 'There's one big difference. Papa is devoted to my mother. He'd never leave her for another woman.' She took a deep breath and spelled out her need. 'I want my husband to feel the same way about me, Jake.'

'I can understand that,' he said easily, as though it didn't personally relate to him.

They walked down the south veranda steps and onto the path leading to the long pergola, which was covered by wisteria. Merlina silently stewed over Jake's offhand reply until she could not hold her tongue any longer.

'I don't want to get married with the escape clause of divorce hanging over my head,' she stated vehemently.

'I understand that, too,' came the tormenting reply.

It said nothing positive to her and she despaired over continuing any kind of relationship with him. It would inevitably tear her apart because in the end she wanted what her parents and brothers and sisters had, and Jake was not about to commit himself to that path.

'So it's best that we stop this right now,' she forced herself to say, her heart breaking at the need to say it.

'Stop what?'

Her feet stamped to a halt at his infuriating lack of sensitivity to her stated position. She tore her arm from his and swung to face him. Although it was still twilight beyond the pergola, the overhanging wisteria created a darkness that made it difficult to read his expression.

'You've met my family. You know what they're like and I'm one of them. So don't pretend you still want to marry me,' she threw at him.

He stood straight and tall and seemed to be regarding her seriously. 'Why do you think I'm pretending?' he asked quietly.

'Because you haven't finished winning what you want yet,' she cried, gesticulating wildly as she drew the picture that made sense of his persistence. 'You want to keep having sex with me. Maybe get me back to working with you. Arrange your life how you like it.'

'Is that what you think of me?' His tone was pained, which upset her even more.

'It's my fault. I know it's my fault. I brought this upon myself, playing that stupid game with your grandfather. And I'm sorry I did it. Sorry I started this whole ball rolling. I should have just walked away instead of…'

'Instead of coming out of the cake to thumb your nose at me and my playboy style of conducting my life,' he supplied matter-of-factly.

'Yes,' she admitted, relieved that he took that at face value, not digging deeply enough to uncover her other motive—the mad wish to make him desire her and make him regret not having found her desirable until it was too late to keep her in his life.

'And your decision to marry my grandfather? Was that to spite me, too, Merlina?'

She shook her head in anguished contrition for her sins. 'I was never going to marry Byron. Your…your reactions to my denial of any further involvement with you amused him and he wanted to continue the fun to see if you'd respond to it. It was obvious there were…issues…between us, and…'

'And you fell in with his plan because…?'

'Because I wanted…' She couldn't say it. Some instinctive pride stopped her from confessing she'd loved him for so long, she'd yearned for him to realise he loved her, too. But it wasn't so. Lust had nothing to do with a forever love. She wildly snatched at the words he'd used. 'Yes, it was to spite you. I tricked you, deceived you, made a fool of you…so you see, you have every reason to want to walk away from me. Let's end it now. Please?'

'Little liar!' he muttered, stepping closer and scooping her body hard against his. 'You wanted me to care. To come to you. You wanted this!' His mouth crashed down on hers, plundering it with an angry passion, wanting to dominate, to drive her into surrendering to him, body and soul.

Her own anger surged into a fierce response, her mind screaming it wasn't right—wasn't fair—that he could stir such powerful feelings and not be the man who would bond with her for the rest of their lives. The savage urge to *make* him feel as she did had her hands thrusting into his hair, wanting to claw into his brain and change his thinking patterns. It plastered her body to his, seeking to merge so completely he could never be a separate entity from her.

He kissed her until her head was spinning and the primitive fever had melted into a river of desire that turned her bones to water. 'You can't deny this, Merlina,' he murmured against her lips.

No, she couldn't, but she desperately wanted to hear other things from him. With a heavy sigh, she dropped her head onto his shoulder, hiding her face against his neck, breathing in the scent of him, wishing they belonged together in every sense.

'As for your engagement to my grandfather...' he went on in a wry tone, rubbing his cheek over her hair. 'I realised that had to be a scam soon after I met your family this afternoon. No way would you have introduced Pop to them as your husband-to-be. I am a far more acceptable son-in law.'

'Only because you worked at it,' she mocked. 'You're not in tune with my family. In the long run—' she lifted her head, steeling herself to look him straight in the eye and lay the challenge on the line '—but you don't have a long run in mind, do you? All you've done since arriving at your grandfather's home the other night...it's about coming out on top. Winning the game. Except this game shouldn't be pushed as far as marriage because that wouldn't be playing fair. Not with me, Jake. And that's why it has to stop.'

He did not rush into a reply. Merlina sensed he was assessing her argument, keeping his gaze locked on hers in a tense determination to reach past her judgement of him and find more vulnerable ground for him to attack. He lifted a hand and gently stroked her fringe back from her forehead as though wanting to feel his way into *her* mind.

'I like your family, Merlina,' he said quietly. 'I like the way it works. It's good. Why did you separate yourself from it, going to Sydney to work?'

The question surprised her. 'I wanted to live my life my way,' she answered without having to think about it. 'What was here seemed very narrow. Too fixed. I found it stultifying when I was in my teens.'

'You wanted to fly on your own wings.'

'Yes.'

'But you've flown the full circle, Merlina, and what it

comes down to is you want what they have—the strong family ties, the belonging to each other, the caring and sharing, the security of knowing they're always going to be there to come to in times of joy or sorrow.'

'They're the good things,' she acknowledged, relieved that he did understand her position, though he wasn't linking himself to it.

'I've never had the experience of a family like yours,' he went on. 'How could I be in tune with it on first meeting, Merlina?'

She'd known it would be impossible. He wasn't Italian, and his family life had been fractured, probably fostering a lack of trust in any attachment, not believing it would last. She guessed that somewhere along the line he'd instinctively shied away from any deep involvement with anyone.

After all, emotions weren't torn apart if he stuck to free-wheeling so better they were kept contained, controlled, while playboy sex answered any physical need. Being hit with her very demonstrative and very *involved* family, it was a wonder he had fit in as well as he had.

'I'd have to say you rose to the challenge at every sticky moment. And I'm grateful to you for…for keeping the evening a happy one, Jake,' she said sincerely. 'I know it was a strain at times.'

'Only at the beginning, Merlina. It took a little while to appreciate the solidity of where you've come from. And I can now appreciate where you want to go.'

'But it's not your way, is it?'

The words spilled out of a well of sadness. Tears pricked her eyes and she tore her gaze from his, not wanting him to see the sheen of moisture or the despair behind it. She looked back at the house that represented the kind of home she wanted to make with Jake, and her heart was thudding like a funeral drum.

'I'm here with you,' he said softly. 'It's where I want to be.'

For now, she thought.

'And I don't want what we have together to end.'

Not yet. The sex was still red-hot.

'Neither do you, Merlina.'

She was too choked up to speak.

He curled his hand around her chin and gently turned her face back to his. Merlina quickly lowered her lashes, knowing he would see the truth in her eyes, the yearning for it never to end. He reinforced *his* truth with a kiss that felt like love, so seductive in its soft caring, any resistance to it was impossible.

She didn't care if it was part of a game-plan in Jake's mind, the intention being to keep her tied to him for at least the immediate future. She wanted to wallow in the feeling he generated…loving her, wanting her. It wasn't too wrong to allow herself this much of him for one more night. Tomorrow, when they were back in Sydney, she would make the break.

Tomorrow…when she could think clearly again.

CHAPTER FOURTEEN

HER father drove them to the airport in his much-loved Alfa sedan. 'It's a very good family car,' he said pointedly to Jake.

Bambinos were still on Angelo Rossi's mind.

Which put them smack in the forefront of Merlina's again.

Her mother sat beside her father, having decided to accompany them despite the early hour in the morning. Clearly it was a show of support for this marriage to go ahead. At the airport terminal, she gave Merlina a big hug and whispered, 'You keep that ring on, Merlina, and work things through with Jake. You're not getting any younger.'

Meaning Jake was possibly her last hope of taking on a proper woman's role.

She gave him a big hug, too, which he not only happily submitted to, he kissed his mother on both cheeks, as well, having no problem at all with adopting the Italian way now that he'd got the hang of it.

'You'll take care of my daughter, Jake?' she appealed.

'I will, Maria,' he promised.

Her parents' blessing for this union had been bestowed. It persuaded Merlina she should give it more time, not be too hasty in deciding it wouldn't go the full distance. Jake had said last night he didn't want it to end. Maybe he did love her and just hadn't recognised the feeling. She wanted it to be so—too much to turn her back on him at this point.

Once they were in the air, flying back to Sydney, she turned to him and said, 'I will come back to work with you, Jake.'

His face broke into a grin of delight. 'Great!' He reached over and squeezed her hand. 'No one can take your place, Merlina. The temporary assistant you brought in drove me into irritable impatience in no time flat.'

'She *was* a skinny blonde.'

'I've suddenly developed a strong partiality to dark-haired, well-fleshed women.'

She raised her eyebrows. 'Big turnaround, Jake.'

'I've seen the light.' His eyes danced wickedly, 'Or more accurately, I've felt the light. Very good feeling. In fact, I can hardly wait to experience it again.'

Which instantly stirred the desire in her to feel him again. Sex with Jake was definitely addictive. Her inner muscles squeezed tight just thinking about it. But since it would be at least another two hours before they reached the privacy of her apartment, she tried to divert her mind into other channels.

'You know I've never met your friends,' she remarked.

'You haven't met mine, either.'

'Okay, we'll hit the social scene this coming weekend. See what you can arrange with your friends and I'll fit mine in with whatever time we have left,' he suggested, happy to oblige.

She still had almost four weeks of vacation ahead of her, but taking it meant she'd be apart from Jake most of the time. 'I'll just take the rest of this week off work, then come back.' She flashed him a grin. 'Save you the aggravation of dealing with my replacement. Though you'll have to pay her off.'

'No problem!' he declared with resounding relief. 'I can even be reasonably civilised toward her if it's only for a few more days. What do you plan on doing with this week?'

It felt surreal chatting about activities outside of work with Jake. She'd never done it before. It hadn't even been two full days since their strictly employer/employee relationship had ended and the meeting with her family had dominated most of that time. Now they were on their own, heading into unchartered territory.

Would their lives mesh easily or would there be snags to make sharing difficult?

Give it time, her mother had advised. *Work things through.*

Her family had been a huge snag and Jake had worked it through. Merlina told herself she had to be open to different experiences, too, and not be so judgemental about his playboy style of having fun. There was nothing wrong with amusing oneself with challenges. She enjoyed rising to them as much as Jake did.

In fact, being with him had opened up her life far more than she would have ever dared to go on her own wings. He had been good for her in lots of ways, spurring her into taking pleasure in her femininity instead of hiding it, giving her tasks that pushed her to work at her full potential, which in turn, had given her confidence in her ability to perform well in any arena. She had grown into the person she'd wanted to be under his influence.

And he'd stopped any alienation from her family, firstly with his timely marriage proposal, then following it up by evading any upsetting ruction at the barbecue party, riding through awkward moments, charming everyone. It meant her family was no barrier in her relationship with him. He'd actually liked being with them. Which was a huge relief.

In fact, the truth was she'd never really hated him. That had simply been a fierce frustration over his playboy approach to everything, including her. But he wasn't playing with her now and she loved him with every atom of her being. Loved him for all he had done for her, loved him for his generosity, his provocative challenges, even his wicked sense of mischief.

However, she did need the big question of having children settled. Jake had not answered it to her satisfaction. He'd said he understood her desire for a family, but so far he had evaded any commitment to being a father. Was it too soon to pin him down on the subject? What they now had together was very new. Perhaps she should give that critical issue more time, too.

Once the plane landed at Mascot, they quickly made their way to the overnight car-park and headed off to Chatswood in the Ferrari. Being in the sports car together, no longer surrounded by people, created its own sense of physical intimacy. Merlina couldn't stop herself from glancing at Jake's hands as they controlled the steering wheel and changed gears, imagining their touch running over her body, so sensitive to her pleasure, so expert in delivering it.

They didn't talk.

At one red traffic light, Jake shot her a searing look that clearly told her he was tense with anticipation, too, wanting what she wanted. Merlina thought how wonderful it was not to have to pretend indifference any more. The need for each other was real, mutual, and urgent.

As soon as Jake parked the car in front of her apartment,

she was out, the door key ready in her hand. Jake paused long enough to get her overnight bag out of the trunk, catching up with her as she opened her front door. He dropped the bag in the living-room. She closed the door and flew into his embrace. They hugged and laughed at the madness that possessed them, the glorious madness of un-inhibited desire running rampant between them.

'Bed this time. Definitely bed,' Jake declared, sweeping her down the hall in his haste to get there.

They pulled off their own clothes, tossing them away in wild abandonment, then leaping onto the bed and revelling in holding each other, being naked together, feeling the muscled strength and the giving softness as they stretched and rolled and entwined, their mouths avidly connecting in increasingly erotic kisses.

'Damn!' Jake muttered as he came up for air. 'Forgot to get out a condom.'

He started lifting himself away from her and she grabbed him back. 'Forget it!' she commanded recklessly, not wanting anything to dull the sensation of his flesh against hers.

'Is it safe?' His eyes stabbed his need to know.

'I don't know. It doesn't matter.'

His brows drew together in a sharp V. 'Of course it matters. You might get pregnant.'

A chill ran through her fevered mind. 'So what if I did?' she challenged. 'We're getting married, aren't we?'

He shook his head. 'We shouldn't risk it. It's too soon to be saddled with a baby, Merlina. Be right back.'

He heaved himself out of her grasp and was off the bed, hunting for the wallet he'd left in his jeans. A sick hollow-ness instantly took up residence in Merlina's stomach. She couldn't lie there waiting for him. He didn't want to risk making a baby with her, didn't want to be saddled with a child. He wanted a bit of plastic stopping that natural process.

She swung her legs off the other side of the bed and stood up, every muscle quivering at the enforced halt to the excitement that had gripped them just a few moments ago. Her skin shivered from the ice cold shards of reason that clamped over the treacherous heat that Jake had fed with his love-making. Except it wasn't love. It was sex without any risk of real commitment.

'What's wrong?' he asked, her move having distracted him from his search.

'We are,' she said flatly.

He frowned, not understanding.

'You don't want children, do you, Jake?' she stated rather than queried.

'I didn't say that, Merlina,' he swiftly retorted. 'I just said it was too soon. Better we get married first, then think about it.'

'How long will you take to think about it?' she mocked. 'A year? Two years? Five? Ten? Until I'm too old to have the family I want?'

'It's only sensible to plan a family,' he argued. 'Not start it with an accidental pregnancy.'

'I'm thirty years old, Jake. Statistically, I'm on the downhill run for giving birth to healthy babies. The later I leave it, the greater the risk of having a child with some handicap.'

'But women are having babies in their forties these days,' he protested as though she was being unreasonable.

'Women who are desperate to have a child before it's too late, and more often than not by working through some program to conceive,' she threw back at him. 'I don't want to be in that position.'

'Fair enough,' he granted, though he was frowning again, not liking this conversation one bit.

She heaved a sigh to relieve the painful tightness in her chest. The dream of marriage to Jake was over. She couldn't hold it together any longer. 'You said *saddled with a child*,' she reminded him. 'You know what that implies, Jake?'

He didn't answer. His eyes probed hers with sharp intensity, suggesting he was uncertain about which way to jump. He was employing the principle of watch and wait.

'You see it as a burden, not a wonderful new life we made together. A life for us to nurture and be part of, sharing in the journey it takes, the adventures and challenges of every new experience. Like Rosa scoring her first goal,' she expounded, sadness sitting on her heart like a lead weight. 'You think that wasn't a golden moment for her parents?'

He cocked his head consideringly. 'I hadn't thought of it like that. But I wasn't thinking burden so much as responsibility, Merlina. Being a parent is not something to take on lightly or carelessly.'

'True. It takes total commitment. And I'm not getting the feeling that you have it in your heart.'

He held up a protesting hand. 'Now don't write me off so fast. I'm getting there.'

She couldn't make herself believe him. It was a delaying tactic. 'Well, when you get there, let me know,' she tossed at him, moving to her clothes cupboard, intending to make herself less vulnerable to any physical persuasion Jake might try.

'What are you doing?' he asked tersely.

'Putting more than a condom between us,' she answered with bitter irony, opening the cupboard and drawing out her scarlet silk dressing gown. 'You might as well get dressed, Jake. I want you to go now.'

'You can't mean that.'

'Yes, I do.' She slipped her arms into the gown and tied it tightly around her waist. Her whole body ached but no way was she going to have sex now.

'Merlina…' He started walking towards her, his arms lifting out in appeal, his eyes burning with purpose.

She swung on him with tigerish ferocity. 'I mean it! Don't come near me, Jake!'

It stunned him into halting.

A torrent of defensive words poured from her mouth. 'All that time working as your personal assistant…you grew into an obsession. That's what it was. An obsession! I couldn't get you out of my mind. I built fantasies around you and when you came for me at your grandfather's home, I wanted the fantasies to become real. But now I'm facing the realities, Jake, and I'm not going to let myself be blinded by fantasies any more.'

'What we feel together is no fantasy,' he shot back at her.

'But that doesn't take any commitment, does it? It's just falling into bed together. Like you did with all the other women in your life. I'm no different.'

'You are!' he insisted vehemently.

'Then prove it to me. Take this ring back.' She twisted it off her finger and held it out to him, her voice shaking with passionate conviction as she punched home her reality. 'It means nothing unless you're committed to having a family with me. You go away and think about it,

Jake. Take as long as you like. But don't offer it to me again unless it comes with total commitment because I will not accept less.'

'Right!' he snapped, snatching the ring from her palm. Without another word he turned away and proceeded to dress with sharp, jerky movements. Angry frustration emanated from him so strongly, Merlina stood stock-still, not daring to move.

Game over and he'd lost, she thought.

But the wretched truth was she'd lost, too.

He straightened up from putting on his shoes and subjected her to a long hard stare. 'I'll win you in the end,' he bit out. 'Don't think I won't, Merlina Rossi.'

Only on my terms, she thought with the same savage determination lacing his words.

He tossed the ruby and diamond ring in the air, caught it and clenched his hand around it in a fierce show of possessiveness, then strode out of the bedroom, out of the apartment, and most probably, out of her life.

CHAPTER FIFTEEN

THE days dragged by.

No word from Jake.

Merlina tried to get her life back on the course she'd set when she'd decided to leave Signature Sounds. Going back to work with Jake was impossible with her ultimatum still hanging fire, and he surely realised that, so she spent hours on her computer, checking out possible positions listed on jobseek.com, jotting down anything that might interest her. She brushed up her résumé, but didn't have the heart to send it out. Not yet.

The weekend came.

No word from Jake.

Was he expecting her to back down, turn up for work on Monday, unable to resist the lure of being with him again? Merlina told herself she was made of sterner stuff. But the nights were hell, lying in the bed she'd shared with him.

She kept herself busy; went shopping, caught up with her girlfriends—lunch with some, drinks at a favourite bar with others—listened to what was happening in their lives, fended off questions about her own, and felt thoroughly miserable the whole time.

Monday came and went.

No word from Jake.

Obviously she could be replaced since he wasn't chasing her to resume being his personal assistant. The baby hurdle was too big for him. And she wasn't about to take it away. If he wanted to be a playboy for the rest of his life, he could take that path all by himself!

She spring-cleaned her apartment, wanting to be so tired she'd drop into deep sleep when she went to bed. It didn't work. Emotional turmoil overrode physical exhaustion. An elusive Jake plagued her dreams.

She started doubting her decision that having a family of her own was more important to her future happiness than being with him. Maybe there would be *no* future happiness anyway, not while she yearned to have Jake at her side. And would that ever end?

What if she didn't have a long life to live? She could be killed in an accident or contract some dreadful illness. There was no guarantee of many years ahead of her. Should she grab what she could have today and not keep thinking about to-morrows? It was tearing her apart, wanting Jake and knowing it would only take a phone call to bring him back to her.

So then he would win.

Did that really matter?

The tormenting questions kept running around her mind. When her telephone rang on Wednesday evening, she pounced on the receiver as though it was a lifeline, hoping it would be Jake calling her.

It wasn't.

It was his grandfather, whom she'd completely forgotten in her intense brooding over Jake.

'My dear Merlina, I was just thinking of you, wondering how the family visit panned out.'

Guilt squirmed through her. 'I'm sorry, Byron. I should have let you know.'

'Oh, I'm sure you've had much more immediate things on your mind,' he rolled out indulgently. 'This is just an old man's curiosity, whetted by the fact I promoted this match with my grandson.'

'I'm afraid the match has come unstuck, Byron,' she wearily confessed.

'No!' He sounded aghast. 'I was so sure… What happened? Your family didn't like him?'

'That isn't the problem. He won their stamp of approval.' She grimaced as she added, 'I'm the problem.'

'What do you mean?'

'I wanted more than he was prepared to give. He isn't exactly eager about tying himself down with parenthood.'

'Ah! The stumbling block. Just give him time, Merlina. After all, he knows you're a woman of steel, not like his bend-with-the-wind mother. Once you took on a responsibility you'd see it through, come what may. He just has to process that knowledge and realise he can trust you to—'

'It's me who doesn't trust him, Byron,' she cried.

'Not trust Jake! Take it from me, Merlina, he's a man of his word. Been like that all his life. Probably because words to him weren't kept by those who should have kept them.'

'But he didn't give his word. He put it off.'

'Hmm…that could relate to the fact that no one in our family did plan parenthood. It just happened, and more times than not, the children were raised by nannies, then shot off to boarding school, responsibility for them passed on to others. I'm inclined to think Jake would take the responsibility of parenthood very seriously.'

Merlina's mind whirled through what Byron had just

told her, relating it to her showdown with Jake. *He* had felt his parents had been saddled with him. *He* had been a burden to them, neither of them taking real responsibility for his upbringing. No sharing in *golden moments*. Being born into a silver spoon family did not mean Jake had been handed everything he wanted.

What happened to a child whose need for real loving was never fulfilled? Had Jake armoured himself against the need? Playboys didn't get hurt. They didn't get involved enough to expose themselves to hurt.

Yet he had involved himself very much with her, even to meeting her family. And he'd liked the way her family worked. It must have been a revelation to him. Even so, his natural instinct had been to shy away from plunging straight into fatherhood. She should have given him more time. He'd gone away, angry with her ultimatum.

Fear of having lost what she might have had, threaded her voice as she said, 'I just don't know where Jake is at, Byron. I told him to think about it but he hasn't come back to me.'

Panic hit her as she realised she should not have taken his ring off. Nor talked about him being an obsession. Stupid pride! She should have said she loved him, should have cared more about *his* concerns instead of judging, sending him away….

'I've made a total mess of this,' she muttered despairingly.

'No, no…I'm sure Jake would be thinking about it,' Byron said soothingly. 'Might be a bit of pride involved, but he's not one to give up on going after what he wants, and there's no doubt in my mind he wants you, Merlina.'

She sighed, desperately hoping that was true.

'Just wait a bit longer,' Byron advised.

She looked down at her very naked left hand and

suddenly remembered that Byron's ring was still in the frozen packet of peas in her refrigerator.

'Come and have afternoon tea with me on Saturday,' he invited. 'We'll make a new plan. I am, when all's said and done, a master of manoeuvres.'

She didn't want to manoeuvre Jake into anything. The thought of any more deception curdled her stomach. She needed to have everything straight with him.

'I'll have my chauffeur pick you up in the Rolls-Royce at two o'clock. Agreed?' Byron pressed.

It was an opportunity to return the diamond engagement ring that had tricked Jake into declaring his desire for her. She wanted to be rid of it. Whatever happened—if anything happened—with Jake in the future, she wanted everything open and aboveboard.

'Yes. Two o'clock will be fine. I'll bring your ring with me,' she said.

'Splendid! I'll look forward to seeing you again, my dear.'

'Thanks, Byron.'

He really was a lovely man. Not only had he given her an insight into Jake's background and his possible motivations, she knew he would be very kind and caring on Saturday. He might also give her more helpful information about his grandson, but if he came up with any schemes to fix the situation, Merlina decided she would not be a party to them.

No more traps.

No boxing anyone in.

If she and Jake were to come together again it had to be their doing, not anyone else's.

There was no word from him on Thursday or Friday. Which meant his silence had lasted for ten days. Eleven by Saturday morning. Surely that had to mean he definitely didn't want to have children. So it was up to her to bridge the ever-widening chasm between them, if she could get her head around giving up on having a family.

In an attempt to cheer herself up a bit, she put on the red dress with the white belt for Byron's afternoon tea. Of course, it reminded her of being a scarlet woman for Jake and buying the ruby and diamond ring together, but she was going to be reminded of everything anyhow, talking to his grandfather about what had happened.

The Rolls-Royce arrived promptly at two o'clock. She was driven in grand style to the Vaucluse mansion. Parked in the driveway and looking very oddly out of place was a large, luxury tourist coach.

'Why is the coach here?' she asked the chauffeur, unable to believe Byron had opened his home and grounds to tourists.

'I understand Mr Byron has a use for it later this evening,' came the discreet reply.

Possibly for collecting guests who were to be taken to a party somewhere, Merlina thought. It was the kind of fun thing Byron would think of doing and it certainly avoided any drink driving charges. She dismissed it from her thoughts as they arrived at the front entrance. The chauffeur ushered her out of the Rolls-Royce and with impeccable timing, Byron's butler opened the front door to welcome her and lead her inside.

'Good afternoon, Harold,' she said with as bright a smile as she could manage.

'A pleasure to see you again, Ms Rossi. Mr Byron is in the main reception room and I am to take you directly there.'

'Thank you.'

His dignity unbent enough to give her a nod of approval with the comment, 'May I say your red dress is very becoming.'

'I'm glad you think so,' she replied, surprised and pleased by the compliment.

He escorted her down the great foyer to the designated room, remarking, 'I believe it's called power dressing, wearing red.'

'Well I'm not into waving a rag at a bull today, Harold,' she said dryly.

'I doubt that will be necessary, Ms Rossi.' His mouth twitched. 'The bull has you very much in his sights.'

'I beg your pardon?'

'You are awaited,' he said, opening the double doors to the reception room with a flourish.

Merlina shot the butler a puzzled look as he waved her forward. He gave her a benign nod and accepting that he was not about to explain himself, she walked on into the room.

It was full of people.

Her feet faltered to a halt.

Her heart slammed around her chest.

She could hardly believe what her eyes were seeing.

The entire Rossi family from Griffith was grouped around Jake and Byron—her parents, her brothers and sisters, their spouses and their children, all of them grinning at her as though this was a surprise party.

Which it most certainly was!

Jake had Mario and Gina's baby son cradled in his arms.

And Rosa was hugging one of his legs—her champion!

'Good afternoon, my dear,' Byron rolled out in his usual charming manner. 'I thought since you'd already had an engagement party in your family home, you should have one here, as well.' He turned to his grandson and like a five-star general directing manoeuvres, waved him to take over. 'You have the floor, Jake.'

'Thanks, Pop.' His dark eyes bored into Merlina's. 'First things first. Proof I have no objection to having a baby. I can handle a baby just fine as Gina and Mario will testify.'

'Taken to it like a duck to water,' Mario chimed in, clapping him on the back.

'And children have an instinct about adults not liking them. Rosa has no problem with me.'

'I'm on Jake's side,' Rosa piped up.

'I'm having him on *my* side for the next soccer game,' Genarro slung at his little cousin.

'Hush, children,' Merlina's mother commanded.

Jake nodded respectfully to her. 'Your mother is in agreement with me that you shouldn't get pregnant until after the wedding, at which time you will have my full co-operation in that particular enterprise.'

There were a few sniggers around the room.

'Your father says a wedding in September will suit everyone,' Jake went on. 'Given you're happy with that date.'

Merlina was totally speechless, amazed by what she was hearing.

Jake had no speech impediment whatsoever. The words kept coming at her. 'I don't know how many children you have in mind for our family, but I figure we should be able to fit in three or four before the healthy birth statistics start worrying you.'

He was willing to have three or four?

Merlina's mind reeled at this whole-hearted embrace of fatherhood.

'I have your family gathered here as witnesses to what I am laying out to you, Merlina, and they have given me to believe they trust my word. The only question left is—' he paused, gathering up a bolt of energy to pierce her heart '—will *you* trust it?'

There was an impassable lump of emotion in her throat. He had gone to so much trouble—bringing her whole family up from Griffith—to prove she could trust him to be all she wanted him to be. Shame at having judged him so meanly brought tears to her eyes. She had been so wrong, not giving him time, linking herself to his other women, turning him away, denying him the love she should have declared because it had to be love for her driving all he'd done to organise this moment of truth.

He passed the baby to Mario, then walked towards her, holding out the ring she'd rejected. 'I'm offering this to you again, Merlina. Will you take it, wear it, knowing that it means all it should mean for our life together?'

Her blurred vision fastened on the glittering engagement ring on his open palm. She reached out, her right hand tremulous as she picked it up, then slid it slowly onto the third finger of her left hand. 'Thank you,' she managed to whisper huskily, her gaze turning up to his in an almost blind pleading for forgiveness. 'I'm sorry I didn't trust you before, Jake.'

'Now is what matters,' he said gruffly, sweeping her into his embrace and holding her tight.

She hid her tear-streaked face on his shoulder as applause broke out and her family gathered around them, throwing out happily approving comments.

'Good man!' from her father.

'And don't you ever take that ring off, Merlina,' from her mother.

'I think I should be appointed master of ceremonies at

the wedding,' Byron slid in. 'Which reminds me. Afternoon tea awaits us in the banquet room. Come everyone. Let us leave these two lovebirds alone. They can feast with us when they're ready.'

Merlina heard them all trooping out amidst laughing remarks to each other, heard the doors closing, then heard Jake teasingly murmur, 'Does this mean I've won, Merlina?'

She sucked in a deep breath to ease her choked up feelings, then lifted her head, wanting him to see that she meant every earnest word she said. 'I won't ever doubt you again, Jake. That's a solemn promise.'

He lifted a hand to tenderly brush the trails of moisture from her cheeks. His eyes were soft and warm. 'You *are* different, Merlina. I've been obsessed with you, too, always seeking a way to know the person you were behind the barricades you put up. My instincts told me you had something I wanted and when the heart of you was finally open to me, it answered the needs I'd buried in my own heart. I'm sorry it took so long for me to see your light for what it truly was. All I knew for certain was I didn't want it to go out.'

'Oh, Jake!' She heaved a rueful sigh. 'I was about ready to set aside having a family, I wanted to be with you so much.'

He shook his head. 'That wouldn't be you, Merlina, and it's all of you I love. I don't want to change anything about you. Not one thing. I want you as my wife, as the mother of my children, as my partner in everything.' He smiled, his dimples deepening with pleasure in her. 'Though you could grow your hair long again. I would like that.'

Love...

He'd said *love*.

And all the rest added up to prove it absolutely.

Merlina's heart swelled with joy as she slid her hands up to link around his neck. 'I love you, too, Jake. I'll grow my hair to whatever length you like and do everything I can to make our life together wonderful.'

Jake saw the golden sparks in her amber eyes and knew he would never tire of seeing them. Merlina Rossi was a very special woman, the best fantasy any man could have, and she was very, very real.

His woman.

He gathered her closer, revelling in the blissful reality of having her beautiful body pressed to his, feeling its giving, loving the sense of her heart beating against his chest, reaching out to his heart and encompassing it with her love, holding it with care because that was what Merlina would do. Always.

And he knew how lucky he was that she had come into his life, how lucky he was to have won her trust. He wanted her to lead him down her path—a path he would never have seen as the best one without her to show him how it could be—a path that led to what a home should encompass.

It was right.

It was good.

With Merlina he felt happier than he'd ever felt in his life and there wasn't a fence in the world that could stop this journey they would take together.

'This marriage and parenthood game is the big one,' he said. 'We're going to meet every challenge and come out on top. Agreed?'

She laughed, her lovely face alight with pleasure in him as she answered, 'Team players...right to the end.'

He kissed her.

She kissed him right back.

They made the perfect team.

Unbeatable.

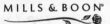

Unwrap three gorgeous men this holiday season!

For three women, the Christmas holidays bring more than just festive cheer – even as they try to escape the holiday celebrations and forget about absent partners or failed relationships.

What they don't realise is that you can't escape love, especially at Christmas time…

On sale 17th November 2006

FREE

4 BOOKS AND A SURPRISE GIFT!

We would like to take this opportunity to thank you for reading this Mills & Boon® book by offering you the chance to take FOUR more specially selected titles from the Modern Romance™ series absolutely FREE! We're also making this offer to introduce you to the benefits of the Mills & Boon® Reader Service™—

> ★ **FREE home delivery**
> ★ **FREE gifts and competitions**
> ★ **FREE monthly Newsletter**
> ★ **Books available before they're in the shops**
> ★ **Exclusive Reader Service offers**

Accepting these FREE books and gift places you under no obligation to buy; you may cancel at any time, even after receiving your free shipment. Simply complete your details below and return the entire page to the address below. You don't even need a stamp!

YES! Please send me 4 free Modern Romance books and a surprise gift. I understand that unless you hear from me, I will receive 6 superb new titles every month for just £2.80 each, postage and packing free. I am under no obligation to purchase any books and may cancel my subscription at any time. The free books and gift will be mine to keep in any case.

P6ZEE

Ms/Mrs/Miss/Mr..............................Initials ....

BLOCK CAPITALS PLEASE

Surname ....

Address ....

....

....Postcode ....

Send this whole page to:

The Reader Service, FREEPOST CN81, Croydon, CR9 3WZ